KU-567-207

# True Animal Tales

# TRUE ANIMAL TALES

by Rolf Harris

Mark Leigh and Mike Lepine

Illustrations by Rolf Harris

Century · London

First published by Century in 1996



First published in the United Kingdom in 1996 by Century Ltd

Random House, 20 Vauxhall Bridge Road,
London SW1V 2SA

Random House Australia (Pty) Ltd
16 Dalmore Drive, Scoresby,
Victoria 3179, Australia

Random House New Zealand Limited
18 Poland Road, Glenfield, Auckland 10, New Zealand

Random House South Africa (Pty) Limited
PO Box 2263, Rosebank 2121, South Africa

Random House UK Limited Reg. No. 954009

ISBN 0 7126 7738 0

A CIP catalogue record for this book is
available from the British Library

Design and make-up by Roger Walker/Graham Harmer

Papers used by Random House UK are natural, recyclable products made from wood grown in sustainable forests. The manufacturing processes conform to the environmental regulations of the country of origin.

Printed and bound by
Mackays of Chatham, plc, Chatham, Kent

# Contents

# Acknowledgements

The authors would like to thank the following people for their invaluable help and assistance:

Suzie Alexander, Jeremy Beadle, Margy Frost, Louise Hartley Davies, Andrea Hatton, Mary and Dennis Hatton, Kathleen Holland, Violet Johnson, Gill and Neville Landau, Mayor Bob Lanier of Houston City Council, Debbie Leigh, Edith and Philip Leigh, Eileen and Harold Lepine, Philippa Hatton-Lepine, Jenny and Ron Lyon, Judy Martin, Karen Pearlman and Tony Peake and Julie Simpson.

The baboon version of *The Great Escape* took place at the Lambton Safari Park in August 1974. The crafty and highly organised monkeys foiled tight security by climbing under the tourist buses and sneaking out of the park past the guards whilst clinging hold of the chassis. The plot was foiled, however, and the ringleaders severely punished. 'From observations, we identified the leaders behind the escape plot,' said Safari Park Manager Dick Howard, 'and seven are now being dispersed to other zoos and parks.'

Howard said that baboons were expert escapologists. When managing a zoo in Holland, he'd personally seen a bunch of baboons luring an antelope into place with a banana. Once the antelope was positioned beside the fence, the baboons jumped on its back and vaulted to freedom.

Fifteen-year-old Matthew Cook from Scunthorpe, Humberside, had just completed a first aid course and had been awarded a St John Ambulance Award and a bronze medal for life-saving.

In May 1996 he had a chance to test his new found skills – on Kimmie, his five-month-old hamster. Matthew found Kimmie lying still on his cage floor and steamed into action. 'I was so relieved when his chest started going up and down and he opened his eyes,' Matthew told a newspaper.

The RSPCA praised Matthew for his perseverence and quick thinking. As for Kimmie, well, after recovering he did what hamsters like doing best – he went straight to sleep.

Twenty-two hamsters made a great escape from a pet shop in Maesteg, South Wales, in January 1989. They slipped out of their cage (probably after causing a distraction) and were later found curled up fast asleep in a nearby greengrocer's – considerably fatter.

Edinburgh Zoo has had trouble in keeping its beavers behind bars! In the past they've managed to burrow under their enclosure to freedom and, the last time they escaped, they literally went 'over the wall'. Beavers can't climb, so they hit on an ingenious plan to scale the heights. They built an extra-large lodge right up against the wall separating them from the outside world and then used it as a ramp to go up and over!

Goldie the golden eagle escaped from London Zoo not once but twice. Caged birds of prey do not have their wings clipped – as Goldie's keeper found to his cost when, in February 1965, he left the aviary door open for a little too long. In a moment Goldie had swooped down and out into the freedom of Regent's Park. Goldie's liberty lasted for ten days during which time he terrorised nearby residents and visitors strolling or relaxing in the park. His exploits were followed by the entire nation on the news and in the newspapers, with daily updates on his progress. Roads in London were brought to a standstill as 5,000 people rushed to see him flying free in Regent's Park and his brave bid for freedom even received a rousing cheer in the House of Commons!

He was eventually captured after being lured by a dead rabbit and pounced on by his keepers. Goldie was returned to the aviary, but ten months later history repeated itself. This time keepers put into action an elaborate plan which included the use of spotlights, two-way radios, nets, lures and the cooperation of the zoo, the police and fire service. Goldie was soon captured and returned. His keeper had, by now, learned his lesson.

When Hurricane Andrew hit Florida in 1992, zoos and wildlife parks reported mass escapes on an unprecedented scale. During the confusion, 4,000 apes and lemurs, 1,000 parrots, 1,000 snakes, 1,000 lizards, 25 ornamental deer, six pumas and three wallabies all broke loose. Many were never recaptured and are thought to be living happily in the wild, having babies and filling the state with some very strange new wildlife!

Walter was a New York cat who climbed out of an apartment window 18 floors up in 1984 to help the window cleaner. Unfortunately, he slipped – but landed in the middle of a bush on the ground below. After dusting himself off and checking he was OK, Walter calmly trotted back into the lobby of his building and went back up to his apartment – by lift this time.

In 1989 Swedish space scientists wanted to see if frogs could mate in weightless conditions (well, they had to do something with their funding). They'd planned an experiment using the European Booster Rocket to send them into orbit but the frogs had other ideas. On the way to the rocket they all escaped (they obviously preferred the lily pad to the launch pad).

Oscar the tabby must have been one of the luckiest cats of all time – or one of the unluckiest, depending on how you look at it. He started his naval career aged one year old on board the German battleship *Bismarck*. When the *Bismarck* was sunk, he was plucked from the waves by the Royal Navy and joined up with the Allies as official ship's cat on the destroyer HMS *Cossack*. This posting lasted just six months. The *Cossack* was torpedoed and sunk, and once again Oscar found himself struggling for survival. The crew of the aircraft carrier *Ark Royal* pulled him out of the sea and adopted him. His stay as ship's cat on the *Ark Royal* was even shorter. Just three days later, the carrier was torpedoed in the Mediterranean. A born survivor, Oscar scrambled on to a piece of wood and was rescued for a third time. That was the end of his seafaring career and, after a brief spot of leave in Gibraltar, he was posted to an Old Sailors' Home in Belfast where he lived out the rest of his days.

A famous escapologist of the Ape World was an orang-utan called Bob. He came to the San Diego Zoo as a 35lb, three-year-old and soon demonstrated a keen interest in the outside world. On his first evening he was caught unravelling the wire mesh of his cage, so keepers moved him to a bigger and stronger cage. This failed to hold him and next morning, astonished keepers found him sitting in the penguin pool, having got through another mesh fence to get there.

Bob had now been nicknamed 'Houdini' by exasperated staff and showed absolutely no interest whatsoever in the behavioural tests that the zoo wanted to conduct. Bob continued to dismantle his cages and started to pick at door locks. All this was done with an enquiring mind – strength being used as a last resort. And this strength was not to be underestimated. In a competition with a former Mr Universe, Bob managed to lift over 500lbs and won effortlessly.

A hippo, bored with life at the zoo, made a break for it, accompanied by his best friend – a goat from the nearby petting zoo. No one was any the wiser until surprised Las Vegas police found the desperate duo strolling down the middle of the highway on the way out of town and quickly foiled the jailbreak.

When the courthouse in Eastland, Texas, was being built in 1897, a horned toad somehow got itself bricked up in the cornerstone along with a bible and a few other commemorative objects from that year. The building was demolished in 1928 to build a larger courthouse and 3,000 people turned up to see County Judge Ed Pritchard open the cornerstone.

Everyone was amazed to see a dusty toad inside and Judge Pritchard held it up by its leg so everyone could get a good look. Just then the leg started to twitch and the judge dropped the toad in shock. It had come back to life after thirty-one years! The toad was christened Old Rip (after Rip van Winkle) and it's said that animal-loving President Coolidge cancelled an appointment to personally come and see him.

When Old Rip finally died, he was placed in a tiny, ornate coffin that can still be seen in the new courthouse.

Labourers working on a building site in Skopje in Yugoslavia adopted a stray cat, but one day it went missing while they were making preparations to cast a new wall. The builders assumed the cat had been adopted by someone and carried on working, making a wooden 'former' from planks and pouring in tons of sand and cement.

The next day the concrete had set and the wood was removed – but embedded in the wall was their stray cat. It had wandered in and become trapped, but survived by squeezing its nose through a crack in the planks to breathe. The cat was carefully chiselled out but the impression left in the wall was kept as a momento of its very lucky escape.

When Jess, a sixteen-year-old Yorkshire terrier-Jack Russell cross got lost, her unerring sense of direction led her – completely the wrong way. Instead of returning to her home in Throckley, Newcastle-upon-Tyne and to the waiting arms of her devoted owner, John Fenwick, Jess set off south, for the bright lights of London! John was heartbroken when there was still no sign of Jess after three weeks. 'It was like a light had gone out of my life,' he said. Jess had been his favourite dog ever since, as a puppy, she'd saved his life by waking him up with her barking when a fire broke out in the house.

Then a miracle happened. John's son Paul spotted Jess on a satellite television show about a stray dog who'd been found wandering the streets of London. He videotaped the show and gave the tape to his dad. 'I knew immediately that it was her, even though they had renamed her Pammie,' he said. 'There's only one Jess!' John and Jess were swiftly reunited – and John has sworn he's never going to let Jess out of his sight again!

In 1499, a brown bear was put on trial in Germany for terrorising the local peasants. He got off on a technicality. According to German law he had the right to be tried by a jury of his peers – that is, a jury composed of twelve other brown bears. No one wanted the job of rounding up the jury . . .

A 6lb Siamese cat called Blackie found himself airborne in 1986. He was resting in his garden in Droxford, near Portsmouth, when a huge bird swooped down, grabbed Blackie and carried him for several yards before his struggles became too great. The RSPB told Blackie's owners that the bird was almost definitely a buzzard.

When John the white mongrel dog was swept away by a 16-metre-high tidal wave, people at the fishing village on Okushiri Island never expected to see him again. But, amazingly, a year later the dog turned up bedraggled but otherwise unhurt. His owner, Naoyuki Lida, had no idea what he'd been up to during the past year. 'John definitely doesn't like water now,' he said, 'but he really loves eating fish.'

The Bratcher family of Artesia, New Mexico, were heartbroken when their mum accidentally knocked down their beloved mongrel dog Brownie in the driveway of their home. Despite protests from three-year-old Toby that, 'Brownie's not dead', they buried him in a nearby pasture. The next day, the family returned from an outing to find Brownie waiting for them on the porch, covered in dirt. He had been knocked into a coma, come to and dug himself out. The family rushed him to a vet and Brownie is now well on the mend. Apparently, the Bratchers have taken to calling him 'Lazarus' after his amazing resurrection.

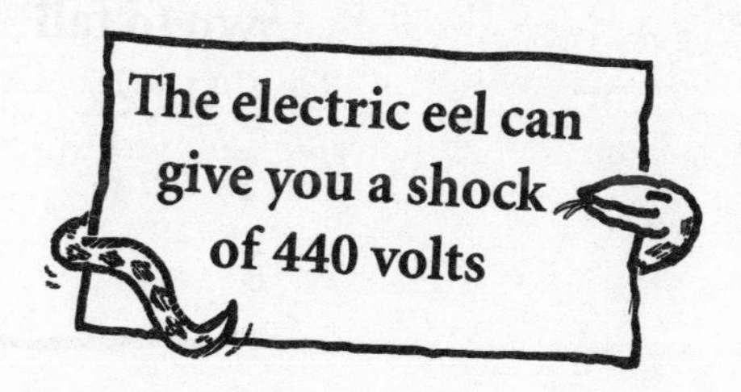


In December 1976, Spook the Alsatian fell overboard from a ferry travelling along the coastline of British Columbia. His owners, Christine and Michael Rowe, were on their way to a new life in Alaska. The couple pleaded for the ferry captain to turn the ship around to look for Spook, but he told them there was no hope. The waters were icy and no one could survive in them for more than a few minutes at best.

Seven months later, the Rowes returned to their old home in Sacremento, California, to visit relations. Christine went to the local dog pound to collect her brother's terrier, which had escaped and been picked up by the dog wardens. As she was being led through the cages to collect the terrier, she couldn't believe her eyes. There, in one of the cages, was Spook. Spook saw her at the same time and howled his head off until he and his mistress were reunited.

The dog warden told Christine that Spook had been picked up wandering the streets just 100 yards from his old home. If no one claimed him, he was due to be put to sleep on the very next day . . .

After his pet falcon Lenny flew the coup, Harry Walker of Belper in Derbyshire didn't hold out much hope of ever finding him again. Half-heartedly, he dialled the local police station to see if they'd had any reports of Lenny. However, by accident, he misdialled and spoke to a family in a nearby street who told him that, by an astounding coincidence, Lenny was perched on their garden fence! Harry raced around and Lenny flew straight to him.

When a Dutch fur farm went bankrupt, the ABN Bank found themselves the confused and unprepared legal owners of 850 furry coypus, an ancient relative of the guinea pig. The cheapest option would have been to destroy them, but the World Society for the Protection of Animals and a Dutch protection society persuaded the bank to think again. Instead, the bank forked out for an all-expenses-paid trip back to Uruguay – where the coypus originally came from – for the 850 little unfortunates. After six weeks in quarantine, the extremely lucky little rodents were released back into the wild.

Thieves broke into John Ashcroft's pigeon loft in Mere Brow, Lancashire, and made off with 62 prized homing pigeons. They obviously hadn't given too much thought to what they were doing though because, within days, all but 19 of the birds had flown home again!

Liz Kaernestam of Austria was horrified when she discovered that the first prize in a Hungarian lottery was a piglet. He seemed destined for the pot – until Liz stepped in. She bought every single ticket in the lottery, won the pig and whisked him away across the border to live with her in Austria!

The fabulously wealthy Saudi Sheik Mohammed al-Fassi has devoted his life and his wealth to helping stray cats. Upset when he heard that stray cats were being killed because no one would care for them, the sheik decided it was his job to step in and save them. He established a luxury home in Florida for over 100 unfortunates, with trained staff on hand to ensure they're happy and healthy. The animal-loving sheik has also been known to clear restaurants out of their entire stock of lobsters to save them from the pot.

When Paula told her German shepherd Mongy to 'fetch!', a hand grenade wasn't what she had in mind. But that was what Mongy brought back with him, and it was live and dangerous! The whole area was cordoned off while bomb disposal experts coaxed the dog into (gently) dropping the grenade and then safely defused it.

In 1994, fishermen in the Kongsfjord Inlet on the Norwegian coast began to realise that something was wrong. A red marker-buoy kept bobbing up and down on the surface of the water like an angler's float. Something was trapped underneath. They raised the alarm and a team of researchers from the nearby Norwegian Polar Institute decided to take a closer look. What they found was a baby white Beluga whale, hopelessly entangled in the buoy's mooring lines. The researchers realised that this bright, curious creature had swum by to investigate the colourful red buoy and got itself trapped. Whales need to surface to breathe, and the rope was pulling it under, tightening around the whale and making its struggles to reach the surface harder with every precious breath. The baby was now on the verge of exhaustion and in danger of drowning.

One of the researchers, Mostad, immediately donned a polar diving suit, grabbed a knife and plunged into the icy waters beside the trapped whale. Once underwater, he saw that the baby was even more tangled up than he'd thought, with the line wrapped around his nose and his flippers. As the whale saw the diver, it began to panic, thrashing and struggling and getting still more tangled. However, after a short while, he somehow seemed to sense that Mostad meant him no harm and held still as the diver cut his way through the cables. Then, with a huge leap, he came free of the wires and burst through the surface beside the rescue boat for a huge gulp of air. After a few more powerful breaths, the baby swam around the researchers' boat and bumped it with his nose, as if to say 'thank you', and then headed back out to sea.

*Baywatch* fan James Thorogood saved his rabbit, Boogedy, from certain death after the rabbit fell into the family's swimming pool. The thirteen-year-old Australian boy pulled Boogedy out and – using the techniques he'd seen on *Baywatch* – gave his pet artificial respiration. Thankfully it worked, and Boogedy came around, to be as lively and as full of mischief as ever.

In Switzerland, Ursula Herberger saved the life of a baby rabbit by giving it a cardiac massage.

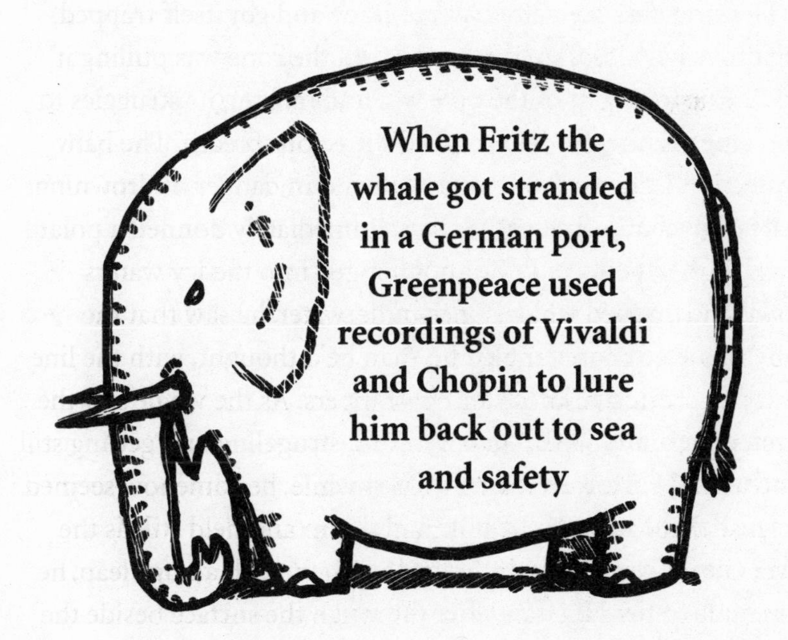

In February 1994, in a remote part of China, a panda fell through the ice on a partially frozen river. Struggling in the freezing water, it was spotted by three young women who jumped in and managed to get it on to the river bank. Other villagers ran to help, hastily lighting a fire to warm the wretched creature. By all accounts, the panda, although completely wild, understood that the people were trying to help it and sat to warm itself by the fire, graciously accepting a huge meal of bamboo, rice, meat and sugar from the excited villagers before strolling off into the woods again.

When the RSPCA and British Telecom failed to help, Eastern Electricity came to the rescue – of a stray tabby that had already spent one night in freezing temperatures on top of a 25-foot telegraph pole in Little Welnetham near Bury St Edmunds.

The stray was seen one day in March 1996 by Nicky Grant as she drove her children to school. It was still there, perched precariously on top of the pole when she went to collect them the same evening, so Nicky called the local branch of the Cat Protection League. Their chairwoman dashed to the scene with a plate of pilchards, but the cat wasn't interested. The RSPCA told her that they had a policy of not helping stranded cats until 48 hours had elapsed and BT refused to send engineers unless they were requested by the RSPCA.

Caring Eastern Electricity, however, sent out a hydraulic crane immediately and would have rescued the cat – were it not for a mechanical failure. In the end, linesman Gary Tarpley climbed the rest of the way up the pole and scooped the cat to safety. She is now being looked after by the Cat Protection League who have named her Hillary – after the first man to climb Everest.

# *Chapter Two*

# BATTY BEASTS

Philip Davis' gelding Rodger just couldn't seem to get comfortable when he fancied a mid-afternoon snooze in the field. Finally, he hit upon a very unusual position which seemed to do the trick – sleeping flat on his back with all four legs straight up in the air!

The sight caused so much confusion and concern to passing motorists that the farmer was eventually forced to erect a large sign on his Farnham, Surrey farm saying: 'Don't worry. This horse is not dead!' Rodger, by all accounts, slept peacefully through the whole rumpus.

A certain breed of goat faints if you startle it. Apparently, 'fainting goats' are now popular pets in the American mid-west and pet owners have even set up two different 'Fainting Goat Associations' – the American Tennessee Fainting Goat Association which publishes its own newsletter, *Nervous News*, and the Iowa Fainting Goat Association. To join, you have to send a photograph of yourself with a flat-out goat! The goats, which arrived in the area in the early 1880s, are now worth up to $600 each. Members of the association once even held a 'fainting goat derby'. This might sound slightly tasteless, but before all the public interest, the species was actually endangered. Now, however, their future is secure and you can be sure that they're very well-loved pets.

A Tennessee farmer who once owned a flock of these fainting goats made a killing when General Patton's tank regiment drove by on manoeuvres in the 1930s. Seeing the tanks go by, the goats all immediately keeled over. The farmer demanded immediate compensation from the army – and got it. After the tanks left, the goats got straight up again!

**Oysters suffer from jetlag! After a change of environment displaced oysters were observed opening their shells at the exact time of the high tide in their original location**

The normally quiet north west London suburb of Burnt Oak was thrown into a state of panic in 1982 by a plague of – hamsters . . . For some reason, a swarm of hamsters took over the Hook Walk council estate, swarming up drainpipes and TV aerial wires into bedrooms and bathrooms. Special hamster shields were put up across letter boxes to stop them flooding in there too. Experts were called in. They declared that the marauding hamsters were descendents of normal hamsters which had escaped and 'gone wild'. Somehow they were resistant to poison and seemed to outsmart the traps. Zoologists spoke in hushed tones of a 'superhamster' – a hamster which could threaten the whole country. Barnet council declared war, bringing in huge tractor mowers in their hunt for the pests. Not one was captured. The noise spooked them and drove them underground, where they still may be to this day . . . Keep a close watch on your lettuce!

Maudie the Labrador has a very unusual talent for finding lost golf balls. She's recovered more than a thousand of them on the South Downs Way at the Pycecombe golfcourse – and can even detect ones buried underground. The golf course buys them back from her at 30p a ball.

Rastus the cat is a real motorcycle enthusiast. Sitting on the handlebars of a 1952 Deluxe Sunbeam motorbike, the intrepid black cat has travelled more than 150,000 miles with his owner, Max Corkhill, who found him as a stray at a New Zealand motorbike enthusiasts' convention. The cat even has his own racing scarf and miniature crash helmet!

Farmer Zhang Liuyou and his family have an unusual guest every time they sit down to watch television – an owl. The owl, which first flew into the family home in Jiangxi province in China in April 1992, regularly comes back to perch on the beams or on the dinner table and watches TV until it's switched off. Apparently, the telly addict owl has even built his nest in the eaves of the house so he doesn't have far to travel to see his favourite programmes!

Delinquent crows are vandalising the Kremlin! The birds apparently love to slide down the shining gold cupolas on top of the Kremlin – as if they were skiing – and their sharp claws are scratching off the gold. Angry Muskovites have taken to playing the sounds of worried crows in an attempt to startle the birds, but they're having too much fun and just continue to ignore the warnings!

Chips the budgie lived up to his name when he flew into a deep-fatfryer at his home in Wootton Bassett, near Swindon. Sandy Smith, Chip's owner, lets her budgie fly freely around the house – even the garden. On this occasion, in March 1996, Chips was flapping round the kitchen when he disappeared. Sandy and her husband Tony thought he might have gone into another room, but when they came down next morning they found Chips staggering around, covered from beak to tail in cooking fat. He was rushed to their local vet where he spent the next 24 hours in an incubator while the oil was carefully and skillfully cleaned from each of his feathers in turn. Chips has now made a full recovery but no one knows why he dived into the deep-fatfryer. Tony Smith can only guess: 'I think he must have mistaken it for a bird bath.'

You'd better take notice of the signs asking you not to use the outdoor pool after dark at the Ritz Carlton Hotel in Colorado. Hotel security cameras have filmed rather large grizzly bears coming down from the mountains to have a leisurely swim in the warm waters . . .

Drink-crazed elephants regularly went on the rampage at an Army supply base in Bengal. They developed a taste for the bottles of rum stored inside and would do anything to get at them, short-circuiting electrified fences with upturned tree trunks and stamping out the fires lit to scare them away. Once inside the base, the elephants would demolish the side of the warehouse and break the necks off the bottles with their trunks, drinking themselves into a completely tipsy state before swaying off into the jungle again. One soldier who dared to try to stop them became the target of an elephant hate campaign. They would break into the base and, before going for the rum, would head straight for his hut and then demolish it!

When the bright lights call you, you've got to go. That's what Spot, an eight-month-old cross-bred sheepdog decided one day in March 1983. He pushed his way to the front of a bus queue and jumped on board a National Express Coach in Cardiff, bound for London. He staked his claim on a front seat and refused to get off, growling at the inspector who tried to entice him away with some choice biscuits. The driver gave up and eventually set off with Spot curled up on the seat behind him. When the coach arrived at Victoria Bus Station, Spot hopped out and disappeared. Half an hour later, just as the coach was about to leave, the young sheepdog bounded on board again and plonked himself down in exactly the same seat, ready to go home. 'I explained what was going on to the passengers and they made a great fuss of him,' said Alan Watkins, the driver. Spot completed the 300-mile round journey and was met back in Cardiff by the RSPCA.

Mountain rescue St Bernard, George, brought shame on his profession – and his breed – when he himself got lost while out searching for two missing climbers. The climbers were found – but George wasn't, and a separate search party had to go out looking for the rescue dog. George was eventually found, wandering about quite unconcerned – and was finally given the boot from his job. It was the eighth time in under two years that this particular St Bernard had got himself lost.

Another dog who brought shame to his profession was Duke the Alsatian. He was the first guard dog to be employed by the Metropolitan police, but, despite his presence, there had been a number of thefts from handbags inside Brixton police station. Detectives tracked down the culprit. It was Duke himself, nosing about in the bags and wolfing down whatever he could cram into his mouth!

Sweetheart, the African tawny eagle, is on the wagon. Keepers at Manor House Wildlife Park, where she lives, noticed that on hot summer days she would break away from the falconry display, swoop over to the cafeteria and share a pint with anyone who happened to be sitting around enjoying one. Her alcoholic adventures led to a *That's Life* film crew coming down to give her a screen test and a taste test. Sweetheart was presented with glasses of lemonade, cider, lager and beer. She knew what she wanted – and went straight for the beer. After the show was broadcast, visitors regularly came to Manor House asking to meet the boozy bird. Now, however, she is off the beer for her own good – but her appearance on *That's Life* is still shown to visitors.

Ostriches in captivity are renowned for swallowing strange objects. A post-mortem on one particular bird showed a stomach containing a spoon, three feet of rope, a clock-key, a camera film, a comb, a pencil, a tyre-valve, a gold necklace, a foreign coin and two and half old pennies in change.

Ossie the ostrich lived at Chester Zoo until 1953 and during his time there, swallowed two padlocks.

Did you also know that contrary to popular belief, ostriches do not bury their heads in the sand?

Black bear cubs are amongst the worst behaved youngsters in the entire animal kingdom and often drive their mothers to distraction! When they're not chewing or pawing up everything in sight, or squabbling with their siblings, they're persistent little mummy's boys, clinging to the she-bear and constantly nagging her for attention. They're also extremely reluctant to strike out for themselves. After two winters looking after the little horrors, mothers often instruct them to climb a tree – and then sneak off while they're busy!

Police sprang into action when they got six 999 calls from Philippa and Gordon O'Neil's home at two in the morning. They raced around to their house and tried for ten minutes to get an answer. When there wasn't one, they feared the worst and broke in through the back door. Philippa woke up to find two policemen in her bedroom, truncheons at the ready. Her cat Chippa had dialled the police by padding on the nine button – then had sat down on the redial and kept getting through to the emergency services!

When Jacob the carrion crow fell out of his nest and needed to be hand-reared, the Weissmann family couldn't have known what a character they were soon to have as a pet. As he grew up, Jacob befriended the family's dachshund Nurmi and would tease her by pecking at her ears and wrestling her with his claws. The Weissmanns suspected that the two might secretly be in love! Jacob even learned to bark like a dog and to roll over to have his tummy tickled. However, the crazy crow wasn't nearly so enamoured of the postman. He'd regularly dive-bomb the unfortunate man, snatch the letters from his hand and then flutter onto the garage roof to open them. Other delinquent tricks Jacob excelled at included stealing spoons from the neighbours, persistently ringing the doorbell and ripping open bags of flour and then rolling in them.

Speedy the rather over-ambitious tortoise was stopped in the fast lane of the M6 motorway – by traffic police. After Speedy's story got on the local news, calls flooded in from people claiming to own him. Police then took the unusual step of holding a special tortoise identity parade at a local nature park with five other tortoises in the line-up. Speedy's real owner, thirteen-year-old Paul Dunn, picked him out straight away.

Phillip Jay and Bridget Taylor thought that life on their canal boat was a little too tranquil, so they got a German shepherd. He livened things up alright – by biting a huge hole in the fibreglass underside and sinking the barge!

Rocky the tabby cat sprang at an annoying housefly – and sailed straight over the eleventh-storey balcony of his home in Lucerne, Switzerland. Miraculously, Rocky survived the fall of over 100 feet with nothing worse than a broken leg and a bruised liver. His owners, Enzo and Silvia de Franco, were deeply ashamed that they had not cat-proofed their balcony and did it while Rocky was away at the vet's.

A fox in California stole 140 pairs of Puma and Reebock running shoes. They'd been left outside a sports centre to air, and the fox was attracted to their salty, sweaty odour. He made dozens and dozens of trips back and forth to his den with the expensive trainers clasped in his mouth, packing it out, floor to ceiling, with his newly discovered treasures. He had almost cleared the lot when he was seen and followed to his hideaway.

A palomino gelding called Butterscotch is the only horse in the world who can drive! His owner, Dr Dorothy Magallon of Louisville, Kentucky, has given him a specially converted red 1960 Lincoln Continental. To get in, Butterscotch simply walks up a drawbridge ramp. Once inside, he pulls the starter lever then puts the gearshift lever into 'drive'. He then steps onto a very big accelerator pedal and he's off down the road! He also has a brake pedal and steers by pressing his nose against the specially padded steering wheel. Best of all, he has a loud airhorn which he can work with his teeth.

According to Dorothy, her horse knows the difference between right and left and is a very safe driver. Despite her assertions, you will be pleased to hear that Butterscotch can't do more than an idle 5 miles an hour in his car and confines his driving to public shows rather than the highway.

Bubbles, a miniature poodle from Miami, Florida, isn't as clever, but she can drive a kids' electric car down the street where she lives.

Two vandal dogs were caught in the act by the police – after they shopped themselves! Rokey the German shepherd cross and Archie the Labrador decided to have some fun and games while their owner, Carol Gilpin, was at work. Unfortunately, the two dogs urged each other onto new heights of naughtiness until they had completely wrecked their owner's flat in Salisbury, Wiltshire, scattering torn bedclothes, furnishings and papers in all directions. As they tore the place up, one of them knocked the phone off the hook and accidentally dialled 999.

A police operator got the call. Asking if anything was wrong, all she could hear was suspicious panting and heavy breathing from the other end, so she immediately despatched a police officer, PC Nick Ryan, to the scene. When PC Ryan arrived, he peered through the letterbox – and saw the flat was a mess. Assuming it had been burgled, he got in contact with Miss Gilpin and she returned home to let him inside.

PC Ryan went first, in case an intruder was still on the premises, and discovered Rokey and Archie lying in a pile of blankets in the bedroom, with the phone off the hook next to them, and big daft grins spread all over their faces.

'They looked so angelic and I was so relieved it was not burglars that I could not tell them off,' their owner said later. 'They are so lovable!'

When Lattie the Labrador went off her food, her owners in Wareham, Massachusetts, took her to the vet. There was definitely something wrong but the vet couldn't identify the strange lump in her stomach. X-rays provided the answer – a 10-inch-long monkey wrench which, tests later showed, had been there about a month. It was safely removed and Lattie recovered her appetite.

If that sounds uncomfortable, then spare a thought for Kizzy, an eighteen-month-old boxer from Llanelli, Dyfed. She had been feeling poorly for some time and the pills prescribed by her vet weren't helping. Her owner sought a second opinion, and vet Richard Gibson performed an exploratory operation, retrieving a 12-inch bread knife from Kizzy's tummy! 'Amazingly, there was no serious damage that we could find, and Kizzy seems to be recovering well,' said the vet.

The novelist Jilly Cooper's dog, Barbara, had an equally strange diet, consuming an assortment of stuffed toys, watch straps, part of a hairdryer and six pairs of her and her husband's shoes.

'Vegetarian Vic' was the nickname given to a cat called Victor who lived at the turn of the century. He hated milk, fish and meat but adored vegetables, especially potatoes, Brussels sprouts, carrots and cauliflower. He was also a fan of fruit, and would eat figs and bananas incessantly. In place of milk Vic would drink coffee (at breakfast), tea (in the afternoon) and cocoa (at bedtime).

A man out doing his Christmas shopping in Warsaw was rushed to hospital with severe concussion in 1976 after a goose fell on him. The shopper had got his just desserts – he was a poultry farmer.

Another act of revenge took place in May 1985 in New Zealand. A wild duck took exception to a hunter taking potshots at him from a boat, so he dived straight at him – knocking him out and leaving the hunter with a broken nose, two black eyes and smashed glasses.

A solitary moose arrived at Green Island, off Canada's Nova Scotia coast, in December 1982, beckoned there by the mating call it had heard from miles away across the frozen tundra. The only problem was that when the moose arrived there wasn't a solitary female moose in sight. He'd been attracted there by the foghorn of the Green Island lighthouse.

In 1969 a Canadian coastguard ship was on patrol in the Arctic when a large male polar bear floated by on an ice floe. The crew leaned over the side and out of portholes to catch a glimpse of the 800lb monster and threw all sorts of foods out for it – peanut butter, toffee, jam, sausages and chocolate. To their delight the bear ate the food. The trouble was, he was still hungry. The crew had nothing left to give him, but the polar bear didn't believe them. He had to check for himself. He stuck his head through one of the portholes and, finding nothing of interest there, decided to climb aboard the ship.

The crew were absolutely terrified as the bear lumbered along the deck. To scare it off they turned the ship's hoses on it. The bear thought they were playing and this just encouraged him to stay. In the end they had to fire distress flares into the sky; this was the only thing that got him off the boat.

Polar bears are very intelligent creatures and rather than risk an open confrontation with a walrus, they'll hide and throw blocks of ice at it. They've also been known to hold their paws over their 'tell-tale' black noses – so seals won't see their would-be killers approaching.

If you're interested, you might like to know that all polar bears are left-handed. Other types of bears can be either right- or left-handed.

While we're still on the subject of polar bears, contrary to what you might think, a polar bear's fur isn't really white. Its hairs are actually transparent and appear white because the light reflects from the inner surface of each hollow hair.

A line of caterpillars two miles long and over thirty feet wide was sighted in the Italian town of Fabriano in June 1982.

Another mass congregation of animals took place in the Chinese town of Huitong in June 1981, where 2,000 frogs fought a pitched battle in a paddy field. This was thought to be the result of a mating dispute and the fighting went on for two hours with bloodthirsty croaking heard for miles around.

Gretel, a Rhode Island Red hen, was adopted by Mrs Tennyson-Leigh who lived in Essex. Gretel lived among four dogs and five cats and got on famously with all of them.

She shared their feeding times, their food and even took the kittens under her wing. But she was friendly to other people as well as other animals, strutting outside to greet the postman and milkman when they arrived.

Mrs Tennyson-Leigh then moved to near Mount's Bay in Cornwall, but the animals soon settled in. Gretel continued to be an active member of the family, keeping watch over the home and waiting patiently for her owner to return. In the evenings, Gretel was a confirmed telly addict and 'knelt down' (if a hen can kneel) to watch it. Another habit Gretel brought with her was her tendency to lay eggs in every conceivable place: on the stairs, on the doormat – even in the cats' baskets.

Gretel's one weakness was for sherry. Mrs Tennyson-Leigh liked a tipple every now and then and Gretel helped herself to the last drops out of the glass as soon as it was put down. During her lifetime, this remarkable hen was a common sight around Mount's Bay. She liked to go shopping with her owner and sat in the back seat of the car between the dogs, looking quite regal as she stared out of the window.

The Stanleyville Steamer was a racehorse with a difference. He was a zebra. His career on the racetrack started when a friend bet horse trainer Jim Papon that it was impossible to train a zebra to do anything. These beasts aren't known for being friendy – and can kick all four legs in the same direction at the same time.

It took two months to train Stanleyville to trot, then three more before he could gallop. In his first race, Stanleyville faced an experienced horse called Cara Winn. He put up a good show but was just beaten. Still, he was the fastest racing zebra in the world (and the only one). His racing colours? Well, black and white of course.

Dudley Duplex was a California kingsnake with a difference; he had two heads. He was presented to the San Diego Zoo in November 1953 and lived there for more than six years.

The biggest problems the zoo had with this two-headed snake occured at feeding time when the heads fought with each other over the same scrap of food – as if they were two separate snakes. Since Dudley, two other two-headed snakes have come to the zoo – all kingsnakes. There's Dudley Duplex II and Nip-and-Tuck. The biggest problem they present to the zoo is having to deal with piles and piles of letters from curious visitors. They're sure they saw a two-headed snake on their last visit . . .

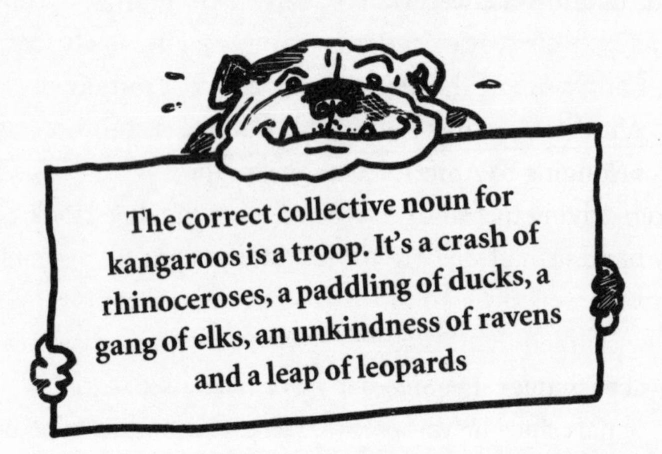


Any animal called Joey the Thug must be one to be treated cautiously, and this Australian boxing kangaroo was no exception. He escaped from his enclosure at the Adelaide Zoo in November 1938 and kept keepers and the zoo authorities at bay for a long while. One brave policeman managed to corner Joey the Thug, but as he approached, mouthing soft words of reassurance, Joey cocked his head to one side and delivered the fiercest uppercut imaginable. The policeman was knocked out cold and Joey was still free.

A few hours later, however, he was successfully recaptured after being spotted wandering around the local shopping area, spoiling for a fight.

In August 1976 Max the schnauzer was put on trial in Texas for breaking and entering. Max was accused of smashing a glass window in a neighbour's house and molesting two pedigree Pekinese who lived there. The owner of the Pekinese, George Milton, took Max to court but the judge ruled there was insufficient evidence that it was Max that broke in, citing the identity parade where Mr Milton had actually picked a poodle from the line-up. The case was dismissed and Max was a free dog.

Another dog in the dock was Bud, the guide dog belonging to American Bill Bowen, who was accused of drunken driving in 1984. Although Bowen had been declared legally blind he had slight peripheral vision, but on the night of his arrest he was stopped for weaving his car all over the road. In court he claimed that Bud had been driving and that he was merely a passenger. The judge questioned how Bud could obey traffic signals since he was colour blind. However, Bowen had an answer for this. He said Bud could distinguish the lights changing and because he knew the sequence, he could obey the signals (he didn't explain how Bud could steer, change gear or reach the pedals).

Half-way through the court case, Bowen came clean and admitted (not to anyone's great surprise) that yes, he had been the one driving. He did tell the court, though, that Bud had been in the passenger seat, barking once for a green light and two for red. Bowen was full of remorse for lying and said he felt ashamed for trying to frame his faithful guide dog.

Despite the fact that you can sometimes smell skunks up to half a mile away, they can make very loving pets!

Joseph Bell, a retired miner of Langley Mill, Nottingham, kept a large dead snail as a dressing-table ornament for three years. In November 1981 he was dusting and accidentally knocked it over – at which point the snail woke up . . .

Sammy, as the snail was named, was returned to the wild and taken to Skegness Sands – where he immediately went into hibernation!

One of the oldest cows in the USA died in February 1979. This was Star, a Wisconsin cow that belonged to Mrs Emma Dahlstrom who runs a dairy farm. Star lived for 39 years – or the equivalent of 234 human years. Her owner tried to register her with the *Guinness Book of Records*, but they couldn't verify the record, saying, 'little is known about bovine longevity'. Mrs Dahlstrom was reported as saying, 'The barn seems so empty now.'

Residents in a ground-floor flat in a Romanian tower block complained time after time about their noisy neighbour and eventually the authorities took notice of them and served an eviction notice.

The neighbour left sheepishly – which was difficult because he was a horse, and an alcoholic one at that! It seems that their neighbour had kept the horse there since he had nowhere else to stable it, and had tried to keep it quiet by giving it copious buckets of beer.

## *Chapter Three*

# Dogged Devotion

When her owner fell off the harbour wall into the sea at Torquay, two-year-old Labrador guide dog Ruby didn't hesitate. She jumped in after her elderly lady owner and pushed her gently towards the harbour steps, keeping her afloat until rescuers arrived.

Albert and Estelle Blondel took their faithful mongrel, Rudi, along on a picnic in the Black Forest whilst on holiday in Germany. They thought he was safely asleep in the back of the car but, unknown to them, Rudi had jumped out and wandered off. Rudi's disappearance wasn't discovered until the couple reached the Belgian border hours later. They waited. Rudi didn't come home. So, almost a year later they set off back to the Black Forest, hardly daring to hope they might find him. For two hours they looked for their previous picnic spot and were on the verge of giving up when they heard an excited barking sound. Rudi came bounding out of the trees to greet them, tail wagging furiously. He had waited faithfully for them to return for him.

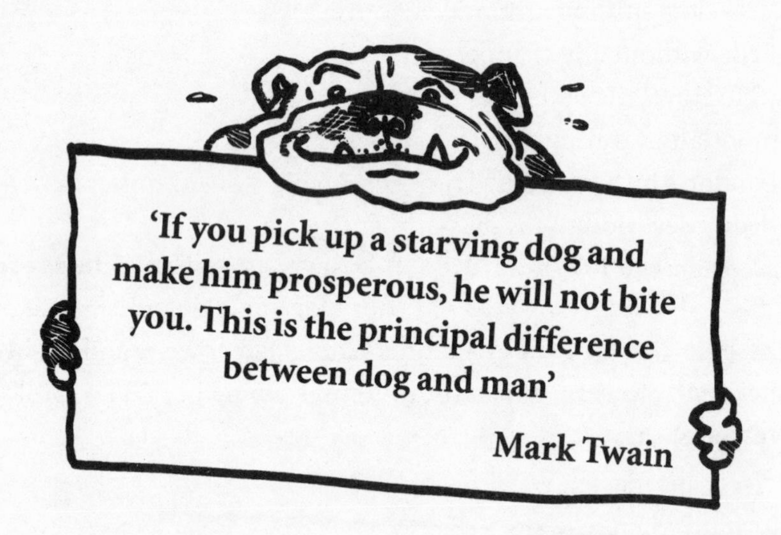


When a collie was packed off by his master in Inverkeithing, Scotland, to go and live with his friend in Calcutta, the faithful hound wasn't having any of it. No sooner had it arrived in Calcutta than it went missing – only to come bounding into its owner's house in Scotland again a few months later! Apparently, it had stowed away on board a ship bound for Dundee and, once back in Scotland, had jumped on board a coastal vessel bound for Inverkeithing!

Bede was an English setter belonging to Louis Heston. The two were the best of friends and went on holiday together. Sadly, on one such trip to Cornwall in 1976, Bede went missing and Mr Heston had to return to his home in Essex, saddened and alone.

Six months later, one of Mr Heston's neighbours told him that he'd seen a similar-looking dog to Bede a few miles away. Louis made his way to the location of this sighting and saw a stray dog, sniffing around. Although it was tired and thin, it was Bede without any shadow of a doubt.

To travel the 300 miles home Bede had walked across moorlands, through many towns and even crossed some of London's busiest roads. The Kennel Club was so impressed by Bede's devotion to his master that they awarded him their top accolade: the 1977 Award for the Most Courageous Dog.

Hector the terrier had spent his life sailing the oceans with his master, William Mante. One day in 1973, Hector didn't turn up when his ship, the SS *Simaloer*, was due to set sail from Vancouver to Japan. Mante waited and waited, but could not miss the tide and eventually had to set sail, leaving Hector behind.

The next morning, Hector turned up at the docks to find the *Simaloer* had already sailed. Sailors watched as the little dog ran up the gangplank of four different ships, walked around their decks, sniffing their cargo then jumping off again. Two days out at sea, the crew of the SS *Hanley* found Hector carefully stowed away in the cargo hold. He was welcomed on board and fed and fussed, but – as the ship neared its destination – he became more and more excited.

The *Hanley* docked in Tokyo and, while it was unloading, the *Simaloer* docked just 300 yards away. Hector jumped over the side and swam out to a sampan carrying his master to shore from the *Simaloer*. The two were reunited in a flurry of hugs and licks.

Somehow, Hector had known where his master was going, known where the SS *Hanley* was going, and hitched a lift for 5,000 miles to be reunited!

In 1940, schoolboy Hugh Brady found a wounded pigeon in the garden of his home in West Virginia. After nursing him back to health he kept him as a pet and put an identity tag on his leg with the number '167'. The following winter, Hugh was suddenly taken ill and was rushed into a specialist hospital. Fortunately, he recovered from his illness but remained in hospital to convalesce. One cold winter's night he was woken by a constant tapping on the window pane. He was too weak to get up so he called the nurse to investigate. When she opened the window a pigeon flew in and landed on the bed. It was Hugh's pet, the '167' tag on its leg confirmed it.

It had flown through the night to be with its owner, to a hospital it had never visited – 200 miles away.

An Irish terrier called Prince was devastated when his owner, Private James Brown of the North Staffordshire Regiment was posted to France in September 1914. James left his dog behind at home in Hammersmith, West London, but the plucky pooch soon went missing – only to reappear a few weeks later alongside his master in the trenches at Armentières.

Private Brown didn't know how Prince found him, but one explanation is that, after running away, Prince got attached to some troops who were also travelling to France. Once on French soil, using a combination of his keen sense of smell and plenty of luck, Prince found his master. The task was made slightly easier by the fact that most of the British soldiers were situated along one long front.

Prince became a hero of the regiment and stayed at his master's side throughout the war.

On the night of 24 August in the year 79, the Roman city of Pompeii was covered by volcanic ash as Mount Vesuvius erupted. Toxic fumes overwhelmed the population and the entire city was buried under thick layers of ash.

When modern-day archaeologists came to excavate the site, they found the remains of a dog, stretched over the body of a little child. He had apparently died sheltering his beloved young master from the volcanic debris raining down from the sky. The dog's name was Delta, but that isn't the end of his story.

Delta was found wearing an elaborate collar with an inscription on it which told not only his name, but his other deeds of heroism. The collar said that Delta's master was a man called Severinus – and that Delta had saved *his* life on three separate occasions. On the first occasion, he had plunged into the sea to save his master from drowning. Then, he had driven off four robbers who had waylaid Severinus, and, finally, he had saved his master from an attack by a ferocious she-wolf. Quite some dog.

The collar also spoke of the heroic dog's love and devotion for Severinus' young son.

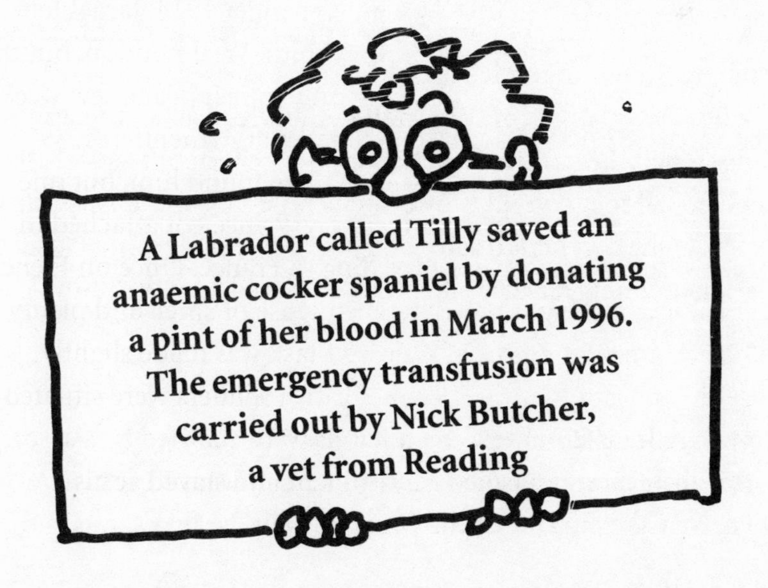

During the First World War, a farmer in Bedfordshire was heartbroken when his favourite horse was called up to serve on the Western Front. He assumed that the horse was as good as dead. Two years later, however, the horse returned to England and was put on sale by the Army. By coincidence, the farmer who bought it was a neighbour of the original owner. Realising it was almost home, the horse escaped and went galloping across to its old home, waking the farmer up in the middle of the night with its joyous neighing and excited clattering of hooves on the cobbled courtyard!

There was no warning. One minute, Daisy the mongrel was dozing in the wheelhouse on board a Norwegian trawler, the next, she was struggling for her life in the pitch black waters of the North Sea. A German U-boat had torpedoed the trawler, literally blowing it to bits and hurling Daisy into the sea. As the survivors congregated together in the water by the light of the burning wreck, Daisy swam over to them and huddled with them. All night, she kept dog-paddling from one crewman to the next, checking they were alright and licking their faces as if telling them not to give up.

Hours later, a British ship spotted the wreckage in the water and rescued the survivors. When they were brought ashore in England, all the rescued trawlermen could talk about was Daisy and how she had kept them going when all hope seemed lost. To mark her courage, Daisy was awarded a medal by the RSPCA.

In the 1920s, the Crown Jewels were guarded by a scruffy little mongrel called Monty at the Tower of London. Owned by the curator of the Crown Jewels, he first came to the

Tower as a tiny puppy, but soon became a tourist attraction in his own right. Visitors fussed over the dog and even members of the Royal Family asked after him. His real hour of fame, however, came when the Crown Jewels' expensive new security system was unveiled before an assembled multitude of journalists from all over the world.

Being a natural ham, Monty immediately took centre stage and paraded about for the journalists – in the middle of the state-of-the-art detector beams. They didn't go off.

Monty had discovered the vital flaw in the system. The beams didn't reach the ground and all a burglar had to do to get his hands on the jewels was simply to crawl under the beams! The system was rapidly adjusted.

The Romeo and Juliet of the dog world were Sultan, a two-year-old Alsatian and Judy, a seven-year-old collie. Whenever Sultan walked past Judy's house in Nottingham, he would look up at the windows and howl – his version of a serenade. After a few seconds Judy would appear at the upstairs window, and howl back. This was the dogs' version of the famous balcony scene.

On one occasion Sultan gave a virtuoso performance which set Judy's heart racing. She couldn't wait to be with him and managed to nudge the window handle with her nose. Unfortunately she decided to jump out to meet him – and fell 20 feet, breaking her front legs. Sultan's barks attracted neighbours and Judy was taken to the PDSA, where both her paws were put in a plaster cast. Sultan came to see Judy while she convalesced at home and they had a beautiful reunion. She's now fully recovered, but the serenading continues.

Sheila Hocken had been blind from birth and Emma had been her faithful black Labrador guide dog for eleven years. In 1978, Sheila had an operation which miraculously restored her sight. However, by a cruel coincidence, Emma started to develop cataracts and not long after, went blind herself. Roles reversed and Sheila devoted herself to looking after Emma – repaying her for the years of loving kindness and assistance she'd given to her owner.

Homing dogs? Hans Roehm of Hamburg came up with a good scam. He sold German shepherds to customers, who were unaware that the dogs were specially trained. At the first opportunity, each dog would make a break for it and go racing back to Hans again! Police, called to investigate, found that one dog had been sold to nine separate customers!

*Chapter Four*

# Animal Helpers

A chacma baboon called Jack was trained by his owner, James Wilde, to operate a railway signalbox at Vitenhase Station in South Africa. After losing his legs in an accident, James apparently became more and more dependent on Jack. The baboon would push him to work in the signalbox, and later learned to help out, graduating from small jobs like sweeping the signalbox with a broom and handing a key for the points to passing train-drivers – to actually operating the signal levers. At first he did this under his owner's supervision, but Jack was so reliable, he'd soon progressed to working the levers by himself. For this, Jack was officially put on the railway payroll, earning 2 cents per day and half a bottle of beer on Saturday.

In 1884, a reporter for the *Cape Argus Weekly* saw Jack in action and wrote an amazed report: 'He puts down the lever, looks around to see that the correct signal is up, then turns around to the train and gravely watches its approach.'

Jack died in 1890 and was buried next to his signalbox, after a career on the railways spanning some nine years – without a single accident.

Believe it or not, Jack wasn't the only baboon on the South African railways! Another baboon called *Jock* worked as a signalman on a small branch line near Pretoria. He received the equivalent of 7p per week and got a whole bottle of beer on Saturdays. Records don't show whether he was susceptible to drinking on duty.

You associate bulls, stags and bears with the Stock Exchange – but not birds. However, one once helped banker Nathan Rothschild to make a 'killing' on the London Stock Exchange. He was able to sell shares at a huge profit when he received news of Wellington's victory at the Battle of Waterloo almost a day before it was public news. His source? A homing pigeon.

I loved the movie *Babe* – but a pig who thinks he's a sheepdog? Surely it couldn't happen in real life . . . could it? Apparently it could . . . and has! Katy Cropper, an award-winning sheepdog trainer, has trained a talented young porker called Rasher to round up sheep with the best of them. After casually mentioning in the local pub that she would love a pig to take to shows, a little bundle duly arrived the next morning in a cardboard box. From the moment he arrived, Rasher made friends with Katy's pack of black and white collies. Now, when they go to work on the farm in Kimble Wick, Buckinghamshire, Rasher goes along too. Unlike the real Babe however, Rasher has more enthusiasm than talent.

Two equally clever pigs belonged to brothers Oliver and Ian Watters on their farm in Llanddewi in Wales. They were trained to round up sheep and did it so well that the brothers later trained their piglets to do the same thing, even entering them in the local sheep dog trials.

Sheep-farmers in parts of the American West were almost going out of business. Coyotes were carrying off almost a quarter of their herds every year and nothing seemed to help – traps, guard dogs, even guard donkeys, the farmers tried them all. Then George and Peggy Bird hit upon an inspired idea – guard llamas. Apparently, male llamas enjoy nothing more than chasing coyotes. At the first sniff of one, they emit a terrifying trumpeting sound and charge the coyote head-on, lashing out with front paws, back paws and teeth. They even spit on the wretched animal for good measure! Coyotes have, needless to say, stopped being a big worry on the Bird farm.

Inviting Jeremiah the gorilla to help judge a local flower-arranging competition was probably not the wisest idea anyone had ever had. As the photographers lined up to film him with a lady judge, Jeremiah grabbed the winning display and ate the entire thing. The Western Lowland gorilla from Bristol Zoo had disgraced himself at an earlier social function by stealing the lady mayoress's shoe and making a point of sticking his nose inside it and sniffing it throughout the entire function, pulling suitably disgusted faces.

In the mid-1980s the West German police force had a pig in its ranks, and a very special pig at that. Her name was Louise and she was a sniffer-pig. Trained to detect drugs and explosives hidden up to five feet beneath the ground, 250lb Louise was an invaluable crimefighter. However, in May 1985 the authorities decided that a police pig was 'not in keeping with the police force's image' – in other words, she would have to go. This set a wave of protests in action for her reinstatement. The dockers in local Hildesheim went on strike, the German Green Party campaigned for her, a petition was circulated and local residents bombarded the press. Louise became a national heroine overnight – *Die Zeit*, the weekly magazine, even took up her case. Swayed by public opinion, the police authorities had no option but to reinstate her. To save face though, she was declared a civil servant rather than a member of the police force.

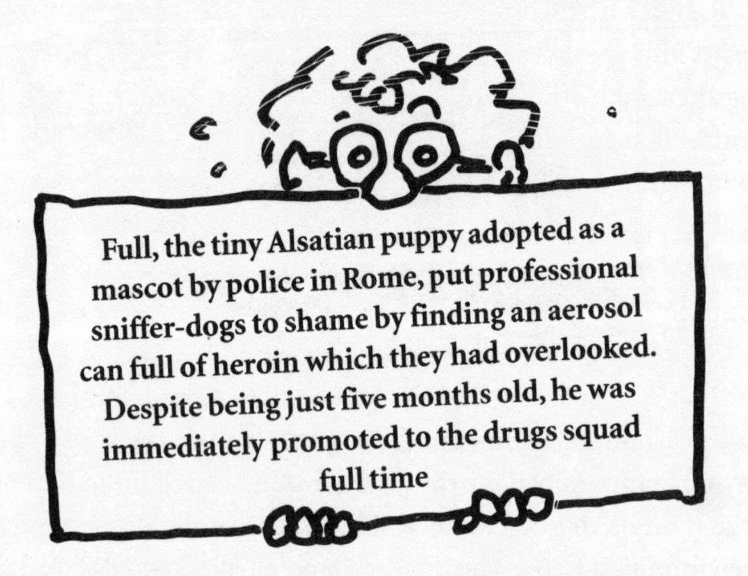


In 1989, a study by Dr E Nathanson concluded that children with Down's syndrome or motor neurone disease would greatly benefit from swimming with dolphins. Joining dolphins in the water somehow helped to increase both the children's ability to learn and their ability to concentrate. Children who swam with dolphins improved up to ten times faster than those taught in special classrooms. Other clinical trials involving some 200 disabled youngsters have confirmed Dr Nathanson's findings.

In 1996, a five-year-old Leicestershire boy who doctors said would be unlikely ever to talk, spoke his first words after swimming with dolphins. Robert Williamson was flown to a specialist therapy centre in Florida after the residents of his home town, Loughborough, generously managed to raise £10,000 for his visit. Before meeting the dolphins, Robert was completely unable to talk or to concentrate on anything for more than a few seconds. After swimming with the friendly dolphins for three weeks, he suddenly gained a vocabulary of 20 words and can now concentrate for a full 40 minutes.

'Robert's first word was "I",' said his mother. 'When we first heard him speak it was brilliant. I just wanted to cry. Robert was mesmerised by the dolphins. He spent 40 minutes a day at the centre. In return for saying something, Robert was allowed to swim with the dolphins. His first words included "teddy bear", "ball", "boat" and "bed", as well as "seaweed", "buddy" and "beer". The centre's specialists say that he will eventually talk properly!'

France now has over twenty Nautical Dog Rescue teams on its coasts! Each consists of a trained life-saver and a Newfoundland dog. The dogs are trained to dive in and rescue swimmers in distress.

Newfoundland dogs are renowned for their swimming abilities and one even saved Napoleon's life. It was 1815 and Napoleon was being smuggled back to France from his exile on the island of Elba. In the darkness, Napoleon slipped on a rock and fell into the sea. Napoleon was a better emperor than he was a swimmer and he panicked, thrashing about in the water and making a rescue almost impossible. Seeing him in difficulty, the ship's dog, a huge Newfoundlander, leaped into the water, grabbed Napoleon by his coat collar and unceremoniously dragged him to safety.

Napoleon recovered, suffering only shock – and made his way to France, to prepare for the Battle of Waterloo.

In 1994, a two-year-old Labrador called Sophie became Britain's first cave rescue dog. A South Wales rescue team taught her how to find her way through the nine miles of twisting passageways in the Dan-yr-Ogof caves complex. Sophie offered obvious advantages as she could squeeze through the narrowest of spaces and had a great nose for finding people. She was equipped with a special torch strapped to her head and carried a pouch with chocolate, a thermal blanket and another torch inside.

The smallest space suits ever made were for monkeys Able and Baker, pioneers in the American space race. Able was a female rhesus monkey and Baker a female spider monkey. The space suits were tiny since each monkey weighed less than one pound. The two astro-apes blasted off from Cape Canaveral on board a Jupiter rocket in May 1959. An hour and a half after lift-off, both monkeys returned safely to earth, strapped in 'space couches' in the rocket's nose cone. They splashed down about 1,500 miles from their take-off point just near Antigua, where they were rescued by US Navy frogmen.

This successful mission proved that it was possible to send an astronaut (albeit a hairy one) into space and return him (or her, in this case) safely to earth.

The first animal to be successfully launched in a sub-orbital flight was a chimp called Ham. In January 1961 he spent 16 minutes in his Redstone rocket (about five minutes weightless), travelling at up to 5,800mph and landing safely 420 miles from his starting point. Ham's epic flight was the last one before man, in the shape of Commander Alan Shepard, undertook the same journey in May of that same year.

Vermona Lundberg had consulted doctors and dentists for years to help treat her dislocated jaw – but none of the experts could seem to help much. Then, unexpected help came in the form of her pet sheltie called Buff. One day he got over-boisterous while playing with Vermona, and whacked her in the face with both paws – clicking the jaw right back into the correct position.

In some parts of Brazil, crime is so rife that guard dogs are now obsolete – people keep guard lions and tigers instead! At least one burglar has been eaten by the beasts, which are described as more ferocious than twelve German shepherds all coming at you.

Guard hamsters? Surely not! But two little hamsters called Hamlet and Smudge did succeed in scaring off two would-be burglars at their home in Weston-Super-Mare. The pair made so much noise with their squeaky wheel that the burglars thought there were people in the house.

Pelorus Jack, a Risso's dolphin, was the sailor's best friend in the treacherous currents and waterways near D'Urville Island off the coast of New Zealand. From 1888 to 1911, Pelorus Jack met and safely piloted almost every boat that came along through the narrow French Pass. The only boat he would not escort was *The Penguin.* A drunk on that boat had once taken a potshot at him! Pelorus Jack's endeavours were acknowledged by the Governor of New Zealand, who issued an order making it illegal to harm any Risso's Dolphin found in the area.

About eighty pilot whales were found stranded by the tide on the Tokerau Beach in New Zealand in 1983. Locals poured water over them to keep their skins wet until the tide came back in and they could escape. Eventually the waters returned and the whales were able to swim off. However, for some reason they all turned back half-way to sea and were soon beached again. As the tide came back in for the second time, a school of dolphins swam up to the shore and guided the whales back out to sea – acting as the pilot whales' pilots, if you like. This time the whales did not return.

Guide dogs first started to be used in Germany just after the First World War, when thousands of men returned from the trenches having been blinded. The idea so impressed Dorothy Eustis, an American dog breeder living in Switzerland, that she not only set up her own school but also started travelling the world to lecture on how guide dogs could be trained. Many experts believe, however, that guide dogs have been around with us for far longer than you might think. A wall painting discovered in the ruins of Pompeii dates from 79AD and seems to show a blind man being lead about by a guide dog!

One blind man in St Petersburgh, Florida, had the same German shepherd guide dog for over twelve years. Unfortunately, as he got older, the dog's eyes also began to fail and he could no longer be used as a guide dog. The owner had become so attached to his dog that he wouldn't replace him – and preferred to stay at home with the dog resting next to him all day. The dog finally went blind, so that the owner couldn't leave the house at all. The solution was simple – give the guide dog a guide dog.

This came in the form of Howdy, a bright young boxer who was trained to lead both the man and his German shepherd in the street. This arrangement worked just fine. Howdy led his owner and kept the sightless dog close to his side, nudging him along as they went to keep him on track. Who said that three's a crowd?

If it wasn't for a ferret, no one would have seen the live TV broadcasts from the Queen's Silver Jubilee in 1977. TV cameras were installed at the Queen Victoria Memorial in front of Buckingham Palace and engineers had to lay the cables through a six-inch underground duct to an outside broadcast unit in St James's Park. To their horror, technicians discovered that the draw wire was missing from the end of the cables. All seemed lost until some bright spark suggested getting a ferret to pull the cables through the duct – all 200 feet of it.

Nipper the ferret was summoned and put into a little harness. Connected to this was a fine nylon thread that was in turn connected to the camera cables. Nipper was carefully placed into the duct, where his keen nostrils detected the familiar aroma of fresh sizzling bacon at the other end. Slowly but surely, a salivating Nipper made his way along the duct, pulling the cables behind him, carefully negotiating a tricky 120-degree bend in the process. After a few nail-biting minutes everyone was happy. The TV cameras were connected up – and Nipper got his bacon.

An anteater named Jimmy served as a mascot for the US Marines in France during the First World War, being picked up by the troops in Central America and joining them in the front line trenches in France. Although a brave and fierce fighter, Jimmy had to be rescued after being outnumbered twenty to one by the enemy who'd overrun his trench. But these marauding invaders weren't German infantry – just rats.

Another anteater who served in the military was called Speedy. Originally from Panama, Speedy served in 1943 with the Sixth Army task forces on the island of Kiriwina in the Pacific.

*Chapter Five*

# Clever Creatures

Determined sheep in South Wales broke through to pastures new by coming up with an ingenious way of beating the sheep and cattle grids penning them in. They took a long run up at them, then at the last moment curled up into a tight ball and rolled over them to the other side!

The Undersecretary for Wales, Ted Rowlands, was clearly upset by this new development. 'We have very ingenious sheep in this area,' he said apologetically. 'We are up against a very sophisticated animal . . .'

Salvatore Monteverde was a useless fisherman, and the butt of numerous jokes in the small Sicilian fishing village where he lived. Fed up with being regarded as a waste of time, Salvatore secretly turned to fishing by illegal means. He threw small explosive charges into the water from his boat and just scooped up the floating bodies of his 'catch' afterwards. To the villagers, it looked like Salvatore's luck had finally changed, as each time he returned to port with a full catch. Then his luck ran out . . .

Early one morning, Salvatore was leaning over the side of his boat; he'd primed his explosive charge and was about to throw it into the ocean. Just then, a large fish leaped out of the water, grabbed the charge in its mouth and swam back under the boat. Salvatore just had time to jump into the water before the charge exploded, sinking his boat. Escaping with his life, he had to swim the two miles back to the Sicilian shoreline, vowing never to fish that way again.

An American tourist with more money than sense asked a local Russian tourist official if he could arrange a wild bear hunt. The greedy official went off to see a dilapidated circus and bought a bear from them. He took the bear to where the hunter was waiting and released it. As the hunter closed in for the kill, a local postman fell off his bike in surprise at seeing the bear. The bear, remembering his circus training, jumped on the bike, started pedalling and made a clean getaway! The last I heard, the American was suing for fraud.

Nim Chimpsky, as if you hadn't guessed, was a chimpanzee. He was taught sign language in an experiment by a professor of psychology at Columbia

University, Herbert Terrace. Herbert wanted to find out whether chimps, like humans, could put words together to form sentences. This all began in 1973 when Nim was just two weeks old. His trainers treated him like a small child and taught him how to make hand signals. In two years, Nim had learned to combine two signs, and a year later, could put three together to make himself understood. Nothing too complicated – like 'me more eat' or 'you tickle me' – but unique for a monkey.

After nearly four years, Nim understood 200 different signs and could use 125 of them. He also used combinations of two or more signs over 20,000 times.

But before Nim became famous, a chimp called Sarah was taught a visual language invented by a psychologist at the University of California in the late 1960s. She used coloured plastic shapes to represent different words, for instance, a red square would mean a banana, a mauve circle would mean an apple. After Sarah got to recognise these shapes, she was taught to construct sentences by putting them together, such as 'Give Sarah Banana'. This method also helped to teach Sarah to distinguish colour and shape, even the concept of 'same' or 'different'.

And then there's the story of Cholmondley the chimpanzee. Cholmondley, who had previously been a pet, escaped from London Zoo shortly after being incarcerated there and did what any human would do. He caught the Number 74 bus. Cholmondley had taken bus rides with his previous owner plenty of times, and could not understand why all the passengers fled screaming and waving their arms about on this particular occasion. He sat there, perplexed, until keepers came to collect him.

The Siamese is generally considered to be the brainiest cat. Fluffy, long-haired cats are generally regarded as the bimbos of the bunch.

In his book, *The Intelligence of Dogs*, Professor Stanley Coren rates Border collies as the smartest, followed by poodles and German shepherds. Dim-wits of the doggy world are bulldogs, basenjis and Afghan hounds. They didn't even make the 120 smartest breeds!

When the MV *Tjoba* capsized and sank in the Rhine in December 1964, Peter, the ship's cat, survived for nearly eight days underwater. He found an air pocket and stayed there until the boat was salvaged from the bottom, emerging hungry but otherwise none the worse for wear.

Horses have always had a strong bond with their riders or drivers and this was clearly demonstrated by Gracie, a dray horse working for the Whitbread Brewery. She daily delivered barrels and crates to pubs in East London and one day, in October 1953, was making a delivery to Shoreditch when she sensed that something wasn't right with her driver. Unguided, Gracie retraced her steps and pulled the dray and its load back to the depot in Clerkenwell. When she arrived she stamped and whinnied so much that workers ran out to see what the fuss was about. There, they saw her driver slumped in his seat. He was rushed to hospital, seriously ill, but survived thanks to Gracie.

There is a real-life Ace Ventura, Pet Detective. He's called John Keane (although he works under the professional name of Sherlock Bones) and he charges up to $200 a day to find missing pets. When Jim Carey – the star of the *Ace Ventura* films – lost his beloved Jack Russell recently, it was 'Sherlock Bones' he turned too. And Sherlock found him!

Most artists work in cramped garrets or studios, but the painter with the most unusual surroundings is Ruby. She works in Phoenix Zoo in Arizona. Well, it's probably not so unusual considering she's an elephant. Ruby was observed by her keepers holding a stick in her trunk, making shapes in the dirt for hours at a time.

She loved doing this and the keepers could see she was getting more and more proficient. One day they gave her some large sheets of cardboard, some paints and brushes and before you could say 'Van Gogh', Ruby had begun to paint.

She's now a celebrated artist at the zoo with a custom-built easel and her own office. Her keepers assist by changing brushes for her and holding a palette where Ruby mixes her colours. She prefers primary colours and often recreates the colours of objects she's encountered earlier in the day. This has caused strong debate among scientists who'd previously been convinced that elephants were colour blind.

Ruby draws great crowds whenever she steps out of her enclosure to paint; one of her works of art has sold for $3,500.

Another pachyderm Picasso was Little Carol. Known as 'the artistic elephant', she was the undoubted star of the San Diego Children's Park. Born in 1966, she soon learned to daub non-toxic paints on to a canvas with a paintbrush – and sign them with a footprint. Some of her best designs have sold for over $100, with the money going towards a fund for the acquisition of animals for the zoo's Wild Animal Park.

In the world of art, Chunky, Mischief, Inky, Rumple and Smokie are beginning to make names for themselves – as moggie Michelangelos. These particular cats are let loose with a blank canvas and plenty of paint, and the impressions they leave have sold for up to £38,000.

The top puss when it comes to painting, though, is a ginger tom named Bootsie. American collectors have paid £50,000 for his works of art.

Ziggy the elephant spent his early years with Ringling Brothers' Circus where he learned to dance and play 'Yes Sir, That's My Baby' on the harmonica. On one occasion the stage collapsed under his weight – but this gave local police an idea. They used Ziggy to knock down the wall of a warehouse which was being used as a store for illegal whisky!

Burt the performing duck can play a Chopin melody by hitting the keys of a toy piano with his beak. He was trained in the US by a company called Animal Behavior Enterprises, who have also been responsible for training such diverse creatures as turkeys, dolphins, reindeer, snakes and even a cow.

Percy the chihuahua belonged to Christine Harrison. She loved him dearly, but one day in 1983 he ran out in the road and was tragically struck down. Christine's father, Bill, put him in a small sack and buried him in the garden. All the family were terribly sad and even Bill's dog Mickey seemed to be grieving for his chum Percy, sitting on the garden path and staring at the little grave.

A few hours later Bill heard sounds of scuffles and whining. Running out into the garden, he saw that Percy's grave had been dug up and the sack containing his body was now empty. What was worse was the sight of Mickey standing over the limp body of little Percy. Bill shouted at Mickey, but then realised that he was licking Percy's face and nuzzling him, performing a canine kiss of life. Bill thought he was imagining things when he saw Percy's body give a little twitch. Then it happened again. Then Percy turned his head slightly and let out a quiet whimper. Percy *was* alive!

Somehow Mickey had detected a glimmer of life in Percy's 'dead' body and had followed his instincts to revive him. Mickey was named Pet of The Year by the animal charity 'Pro-Dog' and Percy's 'resurrection' was national news.

The Russian news agency Tass issued a press release in July 1983 about Batir, a thirteen-year-old elephant with a unique ability. It could talk. That's right. According to the report, a zookeeper reported that he overheard Batir 'talking to himself' and his boss called in top Russian zoologists to investigate. The Communist newspaper *Pravda* reported that the elephant had learned to mimic the comments of zoo visitors. Other people who've studied Batir claim that this isn't the case: he's actually an intelligent animal who talks of his own free will. Whatever the reason, the phrases Batir is alleged to have uttered included 'Have you watered the elephant?' and 'Batir is good'.

Bully Latchford was a dog who got bored with going shopping – so he used to regularly slip his leash and hop aboard the number 93 bus from Wimbledon to ride back home in style!

All the conductors knew him – and Bully knew precisely when to get off. He could sense when the bus had reached the top of a hill on the way back. This was his cue to stand by the door and jump out just a few yards away from his home, where he would sit and wait for his owner to come back.

After a number of serious accidents, German police set up a speed limit of 10km an hour on a particular road and hid cameras to catch the offenders. Their first 'arrest' was an Alsatian, doing twice the speed limit! He was not breathalysed and had no points added to his licence either.

Mr W Bigelow was a seventy-nine-year-old man living in Shawnee, Kansas. In December 1977, he slipped on the concrete path in his back garden, falling heavily. Mr Bigelow couldn't move (he later found out he'd broken his hip), but because he lived alone there was no one to hear his feeble cries, let alone go for help.

No one except his cat Trixy, that was. Trixy was a small dark Abyssinian, and while she couldn't run for help, she did the next best thing – and raised the alarm.

She could see her owner was in pain and helpless, so she jumped up at the outside dinner bell. This had a rope attached but it was still over three feet off the ground. It took Trixy numerous attempts to reach the rope and ring the bell. She fell off a few times in her attempts but eventually got her teeth round the rope and rang it with all her might.

Just when she was about to slip off the rope from exhaustion, a neighbour came running to see what the fuss was all about – and saw Mr Bigelow lying on the path. He was rushed to hospital where he made a full recovery and Trixy was acclaimed as a true life-saver.

So what if your cat likes the *Neighbours* theme? Apparently, there's an otter out there who can't get enough of Beethoven! Whenever musician Henry Merlin sits beside a particular stream and practises his french horn, the otter pops its head out of the water, climbs onto the bank and stands upright to listen in – but apparently it must be Beethoven.

Russian fishermen anchored in the boat on the Black Sea got a shock when a school of dolphins suddenly surrounded their boat and swam around and around them. Deciding that the dolphins wanted them to follow, the fishermen weighed anchor and set off. The dolphins took them to a marker buoy, where a baby dolphin had become hopelessly entangled in fishing nets. The fishermen immediately set to and cut the baby free and the school then escorted the boat back to the precise spot where it had been anchored.

Jack the fox-terrier was addicted to riding the railways. A stray who lived in Lewes in Sussex, Jack would regularly jump on board trains and set off exploring the whole of south east England. In 1881, the *Illustrated Sporting and Dramatic News* recounted one of Jack's typical adventures: 'He arrived from Brighton by train, reaching Steyning at 10.50 where he got out for a minute but then went on by the same train to Henfield. Here he popped into a public house not far from the station where a biscuit was given to him and, after a little walk, he took a later train to West Grinstead where he spent the afternoon, returning to Brighton in time for the last train to Lewes.'

Jack's journeys became legendary, and he was even presented to the Prince and Princess of Wales. The railway gave him a special collar saying, 'I am Jack, the London, Brighton and South Coast Railway Dog. Please give me a drink and I will then go home to Lewes.'

Jack eventually retired to live with Lewes's stationmaster – but still enjoyed the occasional furtive rail journey whenever he could sneak out!

A grizzly bear marks its territory by stretching up to its full height and clawing a mark on a tree. If another bear wants to take over his turf, he measures himself against that mark. If he can reach higher with his claws, the other grizzly takes the hint and moves right along. If he can't match the first grizzly's height, the challenger quickly disappears!

# *Chapter Six*

# HEARTBREAKERS

During 1779 a ship, the *Jonge Thomas*, was en route to the East Indies from Cape Town in South Africa.

A terrible storm blew up and the ship was dashed onto rocks where she began to break up. A local man, Wolraad Woltemade, saw the shipwreck from the shore and, ignoring thoughts of his own safety, rode his horse Prins into the crashing surf again and again, rescuing survivors two or three at a time by getting them to hold on to Prins's mane and tail so he could pull them to safety. Prins helped to rescue fourteen people this way, before the sea became too strong for the exhausted horse and rider.

There were still some people left on the wreck and they panicked. Too many of them tried to cling on to Prins as he waded out one last time. In the treacherous seas, everyone left, including Prins and Wolraad, were swept away and never again seen. A monument in Cape Town, however, is testament to their courageous and daring rescue.

Another horse and rider who carried out a fearless sea rescue were Lionel Howes and Riverton. In February 1957, Lionel was exercising his horse at Sea Point, also in Cape Town. Among the distant waves, Lionel spotted a small boy struggling for his life. Despite the rough seas, Riverton and his rider rode through the breakers, racing to reach the boy before he drowned. Time after time, other people on the beach lost sight of them in the spray, but eventually they reached the boy, who was by now unconscious. They plucked him from the sea and brought him back to shore where he was given the kiss of life and swiftly recovered from his ordeal. In recognition of his daring feat, Riverton was awarded a medal by the South African Society for the Prevention of Cruelty to Animals.

Surely the most faithful of all dogs must be a little Skye terrier called Bobby. As a stray pup, he adopted an elderly Scottish shepherd known to everyone as Auld Jock. The two became inseparable. Then, in 1858, Auld Jock died, and for the next fourteen years Bobby guarded his master's grave day and night, in all weathers. He would only leave the grave once a day to visit Traill's, a local cafe where he and his master used to eat. The kindly cooks would give him some sweet buns and he'd take them back with him to eat beside the grave. Sometimes local children came to play with him and he'd frolic with them amongst the gravestones, before returning to his master's last resting place. His devotion touched the hearts of the people of Edinburgh and they built a special shelter at the graveside for Bobby so that he could keep warm in the bitter Scottish winters. When he eventually succumbed to old age in 1872, he was buried right there in the churchyard beside his beloved master.

Today you can still see Bobby's collar and his dinner bowl in Edinburgh's Huntley Museum, as well as his statue, which is in Candlemaker Row. It's a beautiful carved statue of Bobby, with a large drinking fountain – for dogs!

Dr Elizabura Ueno was a lecturer at the Imperial University in Tokyo and every morning he walked to the nearby Shibuya station to catch the train to work, accompanied by his young Akita dog, Hachiko. Hachiko would then trot back home on his own, but would return to the station in the evening – just before Dr Ueno's train arrived back. He would then greet his master and the two faithful friends would walk home together. This went on for years, as regular as clockwork.

One evening in 1925 Hachiko arrived at the station at his normal time and waited. And waited – until midnight. But Dr Ueno did not appear. Tragically, he had suffered a heart attack that afternoon at the university and died the same day. Eventually Hachiko trotted off home, only to return the next day at the same time.

Hachiko never gave up hoping that his master would return and he loyally made the trip to the station every evening at the same time – for nine years.

As he became a regular sight at Shibuya station, all the commuters took care of him, feeding him snacks and patting him affectionately. When he died in 1934, a statue was erected in his honour at the station. By now Hachiko was a national hero and even appeared on postage stamps.

To commemorate the 50th anniversary of his death, another Akita dog, White Treasure, was made honorary stationmaster for the day, inspecting the ticket offices, the platforms and the travel centre, finally standing to attention in front of Hachiko's statue, the monument to Japan's most famous dog.

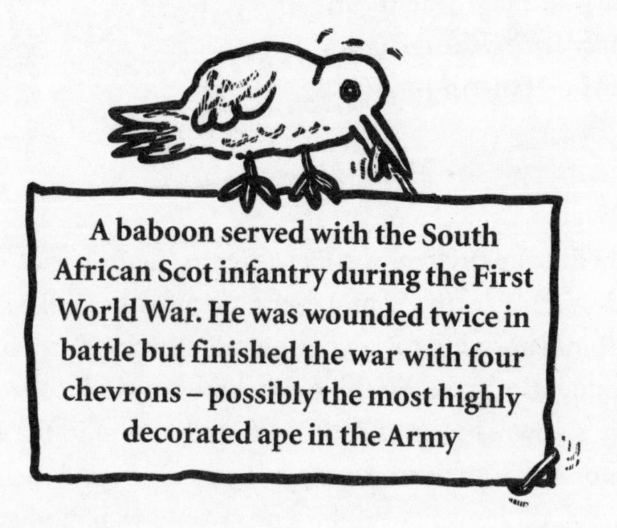


Ken Jones and his wife Mary were wildlife experts who lived on the Cornish coast. When the oil tanker, *Torrey Canyon*, ran aground in 1963 they had their work cut out rescuing seals and seabirds that had been caught up in the enormous oil slick.

One seal pup was taken home by them and they named him Simon. He had swallowed so much oil that it was clear that Simon needed to be cared for in captivity – it would be a long, long time before he could be released to the wild. In the pool that Ken built for him, Simon slowly recuperated. He became very fond of Ken and played boisterously with him like a dog. Shortly after this, Ken and Mary rescued another seal pup that had been washed up on the coast – badly injured and blinded by the oil spill. Ken named her Sally and brought her back to the house. As soon as Simon was introduced to her he immediately seemed to sense that Sally was blind. Simon and Sally became the very best of friends. Simon would act as her eyes, leading her everywhere and helping her to find things.

Unfortunately, about a year later Simon became very ill and had great difficulty breathing. It was clear that he did not have long to live and on the day that he did sadly die, Ken and Mary respectfully laid his body next to the pool. Sally was very distressed and got out of the water to lie next to him – refusing to leave. Eventually Simon's body was taken away, but Sally refused to move – she was rooted to the spot and would not eat. Tragically, after five days of grieving for her dear friend, Sally herself died – of a broken heart.

According to a lovely ancient Chinese legend, the panda was once completely white. A young girl made friends with the white pandas and one day rescued a baby panda from a ravenous leopard. However, in saving the baby, she was badly mauled and died. As a mark of respect, the Chinese say, the giant pandas attended the little girl's funeral and painted their arms and legs black as a sign of respect. As the little girl was buried, the pandas wept, and then wiped their tears away with their paws, leaving big black rings around their eyes. Distraught with grief, they then hung their heads in their hands, turning their ears and noses black too. Pandas have been in mourning for their lost human friend ever since.

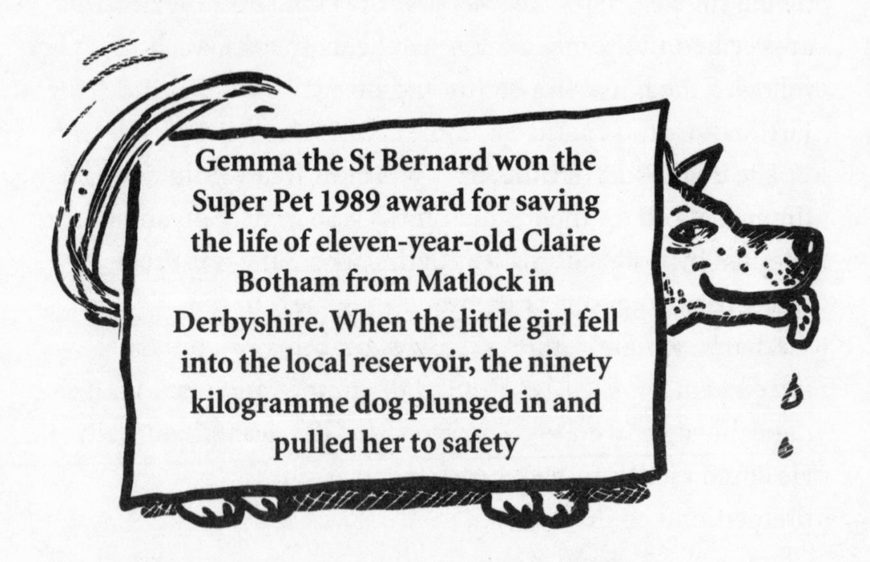


The Emperor Napoleon had just won another great victory in Italy. As night fell, Napoleon strode across the battlefield contemplating the destruction. As he walked, a dog suddenly sprang up from beside the body of its dead master and rushed over to him before bounding back to his master's side and howling with grief. As Napoleon stood there, the dog kept returning to him, as if imploring him to help, and then going back to lick his dead master's hand. Napoleon was stunned and recorded later in his diary, 'No incident on any field of battle ever produced so deep an impression upon me. I involuntarily stopped to contemplate the scene. This man, thought I, had friends in this camp, or in his company; and now he lies forsaken by all except his dog! What a lesson nature here presents through the medium of an animal!'

During a raging fire in offices near London's Fleet Street in 1882, firemen at the scene were alerted by a mongrel dog who kept barking at them and running back and forth towards a locked door. One of the fireman, Dick Tozer, broke down the door and found a girl slumped on the floor, overcome by the smoke. He rescued her and the dog jumped up in appreciation. After the flames had been put out, the dog followed the horse-drawn fire engine back to the Chandos Street Fire Station and curled up in the stables next to the horses.

The dog, a sort of bull terrier, wouldn't leave and followed the firemen about on their duties at the station. He was soon adopted by Dick and his colleagues, who named him 'Chance' since that's how he arrived.

Chance wore a collar inscribed with the wording, *Stop me not, but onward let me jog. For I am Chance, the London Firemen's dog.* Chance proved to be an excellent fireman in his own right. He could race through smoke far more quickly than any of the firemen, and could sniff out injured people in next to no time. Chance even devised a way of gaining access to a burning building by bashing his bottom against a window pane – and then walking in backwards. But apart from demonstrating bravery in fires, Chance also saved a small boy from drowning in the River Thames. Chance jumped in near Lower Thames Street, in the City, and grabbed the boy's coat in his mouth, keeping his head above water until rescuers arrived in a boat.

Firefighting is a very dangerous job and one day Chance's luck ran out. During one incident, part of a wall collapsed on him and he was taken back to the fire station by Dick Tozer. He had been fatally injured and all Dick could do was make him as comfortable as possible. The story goes that while he was being comforted, the fire bell went and Chance made one, last feeble attempt to report for duty, before collapsing in his master's arms.

One of the saddest animal stories I know is that of Gelert, the faithful hunting hound. Gelert was the favourite dog of a 13th-century Welsh prince, Llewelyn the Great. One day, Gelert failed to heed the call to go hunting with his master from their palace on Beddgelert in Caernarvonshire. Regretfully, Llewelyn went hunting without him. On his return later that evening, he was greeted by Gelert, his muzzle covered in blood. The prince thought of his year-old son: could Gelert have harmed him? He rushed to the nursery and found the cradle overturned. There was blood everywhere. Out of his mind with grief and anger, he drew his sword and killed Gelert on the spot. Only then did he hear a faint cry coming from under the upturned cradle. Looking inside he found his son, completely unharmed. Beside him lay the body of an enormous wolf. Gelert had saved his son's life.

This heart-rending outcome moved William Robert Spencer to pen:

*Ah, what was then Llewelyn's pain!*
*For now the truth was clear.*
*His gallant hound the wolf had slain*
*To save Llewelyn's heir . . .*

Did this tragic story really happen? To this day, if you go to Beddgelert, which means in Welsh 'grave of Gelert', you can still see the cairn of stones Prince Llewelyn is supposed to have built in tribute to the most faithful dog of all ...

There are other versions of this story around the world. In France a greyhound and a falcon guard the child against a snake – with the same sad consequences. Indians relate a similar story – also with a hound left in charge.

There was only one survivor of the Battle of the Little Big Horn, when the US 7th Cavalry, under General George Custer, were massacred in June 1876. This was a captain's horse which, ironically, had an Indian name, Comanche. Comanche recovered from seven bullet and arrow wounds and was taken back to Fort Lincoln, Dakota. A special order was issued preventing anyone from riding him ever again, in tribute to the men who had died. Comanche was allowed to wander freely and was paraded at all ceremonies. He died in 1903, aged 30 – the lone witness to the worst defeat the US cavalry had ever suffered.

# *Chapter Seven*

# BIG SOFTIES

Maybe the owl and the pussycat really did put to sea in a beautiful pea green boat after all. Personally, I always thought that there'd be fur and feathers flying everywhere, but a recent story from the Twyford Wildlife Centre at Evesham has made me think again. Bjork, the little eagle owlet, had been sent to Coventry by her fellow owls and was slowly pining away. Then David and Michelle Buncle, who run the centre, came up with a very weird plan. Their cat, Chief, had just had kittens, so David and Michelle smuggled Bjork the owlet into the cat basket!

'It was amazing,' said David. 'The mother took to the owl as if she was another kitten. Bjork and the kittens play games and even sleep together!'

Although the one-ton African black rhinoceros looks like one of the most fearsome and ferocious animals on the veldt, he is in fact a huge softie. People who have worked with black rhinos say that they are the most easily tamed animals in all of Africa. They'll eat out of your hand and even trot over to see you when you call them – because there's nothing they love more than having their ears rubbed.

The Hungarian couple who bought an adorable fluffy white puppy at a street market in Budapest were delighted with their new purchase. They lavished every attention on it and even started to train it. Despite this, the puppy began to get quite vicious and developed a ravenous appetite, eating the couple out of house and home. Taking the puppy for its vaccinations, they were told by a startled vet that what they had wasn't a puppy at all – but a polar bear cub! The cub had probably come from one of the zoos which closed down in the East when Communism fell.

Bilbo the rather large and overweight fluffy ginger tom started a mass panic when he went out for a stroll along a canal towpath in Winchmore Hill. People out walking mistook him for an escaped lioness. Thirty police officers rushed to the scene, a police helicopter was scrambled and marksmen from London Zoo stood by armed with tranquilliser guns. Police with megaphones toured the area warning residents to stay indoors and children in a local school were kept in after class for fear of the escaped beast.

Bilbo's owner, Carmel Jarvis, said the whole thing was ridiculous: 'He's not ferocious at all. He once brought a sponge cake in through the cat flap, but that's about all!'

Laddie and Boy, police sniffer dogs, got on the wrong side of the law during a drugs raid in the Midlands in 1967. While their handler interrogated two suspects at the scene, the dogs made a spectacle of themselves by lying down in front of the suspects and begging to be tickled. After being fussed over for a while, they eventually curled up next to each other and fell asleep in front of the fire. To add insult to injury, when one of their handlers went to handcuff the suspects, his dog snarled at him and the other dog jumped up and bit his handler on the leg.

Needless to say, both dogs were looking for new jobs shortly afterwards.

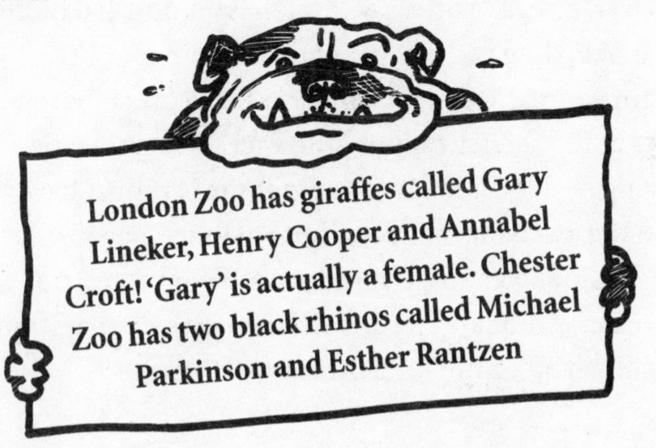


When five-year-old Levan Merritt fell into the gorilla enclosure at Jersey Zoo and was knocked unconscious, spectators could only watch in horror as the little boy was approached by Jambo, a massive silver-backed gorilla. However, instead of attacking the child, Jambo straddled him, sniffed him all over and then ever so gently touched him to try to wake him up.

Obviously concerned, Jambo then put himself between the boy and the other wild gorillas in the enclosure. The whole incident was captured on videotape and made headlines world wide. Jambo received thousands of letters and gifts, including one from the US Army. In honour of his kindness, the BBC's *Wildlife* magazine began their annual Jambo Award.

A similar incident took place recently at the Brookfield Zoo in Illinois but this time the heroine was a female western lowland gorilla named Binti Jua. In August 1996 Binti was playing in the gorilla enclosure with her baby when a three-year-old boy climbed over the guard rail and fell in. Onlookers watched horrified as the boy lay injured on the ground but Binti ambled over and gently picked the boy up, cradling him in her strong arms and carrying him over to the doorway where zoo staff were anxiously waiting.

Oscar, a feral Scottish wildcat, has an unusual best friend – a pet white rat! They both live together at the Mellerstain Animal Welfare Centre on the Scottish border. Assistants at the shelter thought the worst when they first saw the rat lying beside Oscar. 'We thought the cat must have killed him,' said the assistant manager, 'but when we gave the rat a poke, he just looked at us, blinked a couple of times, pulled the cat's tail around him and went back to sleep! It's very strange – because the cat spits and scratches at us!'

When American President Theodore Roosevelt refused to shoot a defenceless bear cub while out hunting in 1902, he unwittingly gave rise to the most popular toy of all time. When the story got out, a cartoonist drew a cynical cartoon about the incident. In New York, a toymaker named Morris Michtom saw the cartoon and it gave him an idea. He made a stuffed bear cub and, to his delight, saw it was snatched up immediately by an eager purchaser in his Brooklyn Candy Store. Being a canny fella, Morris then wrote to President Roosevelt asking for permission to market the new toy under the president's nickname. His nickname, of course, was Teddy – and the teddy bear was born.

Ada the pointer stepped in when a quartet of two-day-old kittens lost their mother. Ada had always loved cats and found the four tiny kittens – Mau, Tiger, Pen and Donny – absolutely irresistible. She climbed into their cat basket and immediately began to mother them. They took to her straight away too – and treated her just as badly as they'd treat any mother cat, clambering about and demanding food all the time!

If such a combination sounds unlikely, consider the odd couple at Maitland's Cogliata Zoo in Italy. Kikko the lion grew up from a tiny cub alongside Neve the spitz mongrel and the two became great friends. However, when Neve stopped growing, Kikko didn't and the keepers decided to separate them for safety's sake. It didn't work. Kikko and Neve pined for each other so badly that, in the end, the keepers relented and let them get back together. After that, Neve was a regular visitor to Kikko's enclosure, playing boisterous games, curling up together and taking a nap and even eating out of the same dish!

A bunch of farmers were horrified when a vixen gave birth to a litter of pups close to their land, and set off to wipe the family out. The wary vixen successfully escaped with all of her cubs – except one. The poor youngster left behind was as small as a mouse and still hadn't opened her eyes. One of the farmers' wives grabbed the baby from under the men's noses and took it home with her to the farmhouse. The fox cub was so tiny that there seemed to be no hope that it would survive, but – in desperation – the farmer's wife slipped the cub, whom she nicknamed Bonnie, into a litter of newborn kittens. It worked.

Merle, the mother cat, took to the fox cub as if it were one of her own and suckled and nurtured her. The cub grew up with the kittens, tussling and romping with them around the farmyard before being allowed to go back into the wild.

An orphaned baby koala was raised by Mr and Mrs Faulkner of Northern Queensland in the late 1960s. They fed their new baby with milk from a bottle and fresh gum leaves, but he would only go to sleep in the arms of a large toy teddy bear.

Blondie the Labrador had a very unusual playmate – a seal called Sealie. Blondie's owner, Carin Mathieson, found Sealie abandoned as a pup on a beach near Angelholm, Sweden, and nursed her back to health before returning her to the ocean. Sealie hung around for a while, swimming alongside Carin each day, and then disappeared for the winter. The next summer, as a fully grown seal, she returned to her human and canine friends, Carin and Blondie.

People walking along the shore were astonished to see the dog and the seal frolicking together in the water, racing and tumbling in the waves, diving and surfacing and barking at each other. While the locals were thrilled, however, visiting fishermen complained that Sealie was eating their catches and made threats against her.

The villagers were outraged and petitioned the town council for help. The council were only too pleased to assist and granted Sealie an official fishing licence, giving her as much right to fish in Angelholm as any human angler.

Alfred was a 490lb gorilla who lived in Bristol Zoo from 1930 until 1948. His preserved body is kept at the Bristol Museum and he was so loved by everyone in the city that a bronze bust was commissioned in his memory. Despite his bulk and sometimes fierce appearance, Albert was actually terrified of air raids. Bristol was the scene of some heavy bombing during the Second World War and at the first sound of air raid sirens, Albert would try to hide from the German aircraft by crouching in the corner of his cage and covering himself with straw.

**Killer whales are neither killers – nor whales. There's no account of them wilfully attacking people and they're actually a rather big breed of dolphin**

Highway planners building a major new motorway into Zurich fed the road down and through a huge tunnel along part of the route. The reason – to allow hares to cross the road safely over the top of the tunnel.

You'd think the odds would all be stacked against Lottie the Rottie. The Rottweiler had been badly abused by previous owners and had lost an ear. Yet, despite this, she has such a wonderful nature that she has become a registered PAT dog, visiting the sick and elderly, and has raised large amounts of money for charity. In 1994, Lottie won the Spillers Bonio Award for Britain's most marvellous dog!

During the war, Jackie, a brown and white mongrel, took it upon himself to ensure that the kittens in his house were safe. Whenever the air raid sirens went, he'd scoop the kittens up in his mouth and carry them down to the shelter!

Voytek the Syrian bear was the mascot of the 2nd Polish Transport Company in Palestine during the Second World War. Discovered as a cub lying beside the road, Voytek as much adopted Lance Corporal Peter Prendys as the Company adopted him. As he grew, he remained completely tame and even cried like a baby when his master left him alone – but the big bear still got into numerous scrapes. On one occasion, he managed to raid the clothesline belonging to some women soldiers and paraded around the camp with their underwear wrapped around his head. Another time, he stole a bottle of white wine and, in a moment of drunken bravado, broke into the NAAFI and ate himself stupid on jam, honey and fruit until he passed out in a heap. He delighted in playing tricks and loved to scare female bathers by swimming underwater and then surfacing unexpectedly in their midst and bellowing fiercely.

Despite Peter's best efforts, Voytek kept getting into mischief. He learned how to use the showers and a guard had to be posted to stop him using up the entire water supply! He did redeem himself shortly afterwards, by catching an Arab spy in a tent. For this heroic deed, he was given two bottles of his favourite beer and allowed to use the showers to his heart's content!

It was when the Company finally saw action, during the Italian Campaign, that Voytek started to get serious. Seeing a truck being unloaded, he wandered up and held his paws out just like a regular soldier and from then on regularly helped to unload boxes of ammunition and even artillery shells.

In 1945, Voytek joined the victory parade like a regular veteran, marching through the streets of Glasgow where thousands cheered him on!

They saw him coming. And they sold him a pup. A travelling gypsy fair sold a lovely pedigree puppy to Bruno Alti in Brescia, northern Italy. A month later, perturbed by its ravenous appetite and lack of any barking ability, he took it to be checked over by a vet. The vet stared at him, stared at the puppy and made an almost instant diagnosis. The puppy was, in fact, a lion cub.

When a hungry tabby kitten accidentally strayed into the bear enclosure at Wildlife Images Animal Refuge in Oregon, staff were horrified. The pen was occupied by a 40-stone fully grown grizzly bear called Griz. Worse, the kitten was sniffing around the grizzly's dinner plate…

As Manager Davy Siddon watched, the fully grown grizzly approached the little kitten and then did something quite extraordinary. He pulled a piece of chicken off of his own plate and offered it to the kitten.

The friendship offering was obviously accepted because, after that, the grizzly and the kitten became firm friends, eating, sleeping and playing together in the bear pen! The only explanation refuge staff could come up with was that Griz, like the kitten, had been found wandering as a baby after his mother and sister had been killed by a train. He recognised the kitten's plight and decided to lend a helping paw.

This year, I met Dave and Griz during filming for a BBC TV special *Animal Hospital Goes West* and was lucky enough to see the huge bear and the kitten, now a fully grown cat, wandering around together. They are never far apart and at one stage the cat allowed itself to be picked up and carried for quite a distance gripped in the bear's mouth.

*Chapter Eight*

# Feathered Friends

Traffic was brought to a complete standstill in busy Kensington High Street in the summer of 1993 when astonished motorists found their way blocked by a mother duck leading a string of baby ducks. Unconcerned by all the cars and commotion, mum and her ducklings were biding their time, slowly waddling up the high street in single file. Two policemen managed to coax the family into a box and set them free again in the safer surroundings of Kensington Palace Gardens.

The chances of a golfer getting a hole in one are remote – but then so are the odds for a golfer hitting a bird in flight. But that's what a mystery golfer at the Bridgnorth Club did in March 1996. The ball hit a sparrowhawk as it circled lazily over the fifteenth green, knocking it to the ground – and knocking it out. The bird was handed to the RSPCA centre in Much Wenlock, where he was named Harry. Harry was hand-fed for six days before being fit enough to be returned to the wild. RSPCA spokesman Dave Taylor said that Harry, 'was pretty concussed when he came to us and it took plenty of tender loving care to get him back to his normal self.'

It's not recorded whether the golfer's stroke was a 'birdie'.

A month earlier there was a role reversal, when Mrs Karen

Giles of Sydney was hit by a flying golfball – dropped on her by a passing crow. Mrs Giles was in the playground at the nursery school where she teaches when she and a colleague spotted three crows flying overhead. She noticed that one of the birds was carrying something round and white – but all she remembers next is feeling a sudden pain just above the eye which nearly knocked her over. Thankfully, apart from severe bruising and a small cut, Mrs Giles was otherwise unhurt. The nurse at the hospital was probably more surprised; she entered in the admissions book, 'Patient struck in left eye by golfball... dropped by passing crow.'

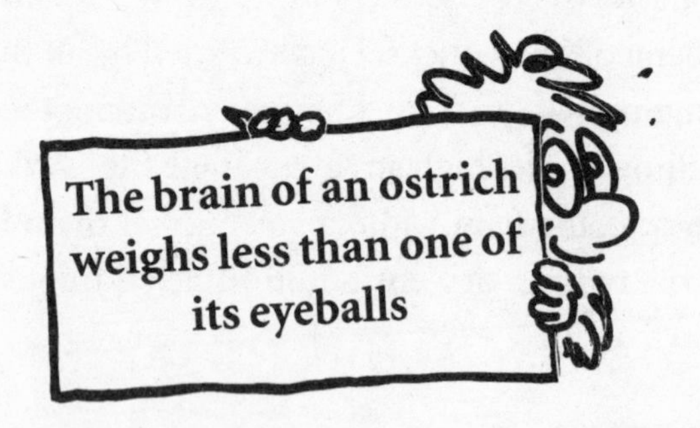


The burglar who had been casing Mrs Mary Humphrey's bungalow in Wakefield, West Yorkshire, got the shock of his life. After watching the house to make sure the pensioner didn't have a guard dog, he started in through a window – only to be met by the sound of a frenzied Rottweiler! The burglar froze in panic and Mrs Humphrey gave him three heftly clouts with her walking stick before he recovered and fled into the night – unaware that the 'frenzied Rottweiler' was none other than Billy the cockatiel!

Apart from his talented guard dog impression Billy, who apparently loves eating dog biscuits, is now working on an even more effective burglar deterrent – the sound of a police car siren!

Bert the vulture is a bit of a failure when it comes to taking to the skies – he suffers from vertigo. Bert was hand-reared – at Whipsnade Wild Animal Park in Bedfordshire, where he never flew higher than about ten feet. His trainer is keeper Andy Reeve who spends time running alongside Bert, flapping his arms and shouting words of encouragement to try to get him to soar higher and higher.

In the wilds of Africa, one-year-old Bert would already know the basics of taking off and landing by watching his parents, and would be ready to leave the nest and find his own food.

Although training Bert to overcome his fear of heights is hard work, Andy says, 'Everyone likes him because he's such an easy-going character. He is wonderful to work with.' However, when commenting on his progress in May 1996, Andy said, 'The way things are going, I can see it taking five years...'

Update from *Animal Hospital on the Hoof* (June 1996): Bert has now made two descents from a hot-air balloon, one from 50 feet and one from 150 feet!

You could have knocked pigeon fancier David Dougal over with a feather when he discovered that not one but two of his favourite racing pigeons had flown the coop for the warmer climes of Casablanca. The first bird went missing on a cross-channel race between its home in Hexham, Northumberland, and Beauvais in France. A while later, Mr

Dougal got a letter from Casablanca. The bird had turned up there, 3,000 miles away, in a pigeon loft belonging to Essofi Mohammed. Three months later a second bird – a nephew of the first – also went missing. Amazingly, he turned up at Mr Mohammed's pigeon loft too!

'There's probably more chance of winning the National Lottery than of that happening,' said a stunned Mr Dougal. 'He was only a few weeks old and had just learned to fly when he took off from the loft. It's like he had a sixth sense about where the other one was…'

The Missing Budgie Bureau was founded by Mr Alan Moon, secretary of a local budgerigar society. Thirty years on, the Hartlepool-based bureau has successfully reunited thousands of lost birds with their owners. Mr Moon's tip to any budgerigar fanciers worried about losing their birds is to teach them to recite their telephone numbers.

The railway station at Berne-Stoeckacker in Switzerland was thrown into chaos when trains kept setting off while passengers were still getting on board. Furious rows erupted between the stationmaster and the drivers. The drivers claimed they'd clearly heard the stationmaster's whistle telling them to go. The stationmaster denied it. Finally, the real culprit was discovered – a gifted blackbird who could mimic the stationmaster's whistle perfectly. The stationmaster threw away his whistle and switched to hand signals from then on.

Pastor Patrick, the bible-bashing budgie form Texas, sits on his church porch saying things like 'Praise be to Jesus' and 'Walk in the light'. His owner, the Reverend James Johnson, said that Pastor Patrick was a very popular preacher, because he wasn't half so long-winded as most evangelists!

Bozo the cockatoo was the surprise witness in an Argentinian divorce case. The sharp-eared bird had been listening in while his master, Carlos DeGambo, was enjoying a fling with his secretary. Shown a picture of the secretary, Bozo squawked, 'Honeybun I love you!' and 'Ruby loves Carlos!' and then began to giggle in a high-pitched female voice. Mr DeGambo's lawyer was outraged at the cockatoo's testimony and demanded that it be stricken from the record, but the judge let it stand and granted a divorce!

Homing pigeons are increasingly turning to a life of crime. Car thieves in Taiwan are using them to collect ransoms from the car owners. They leave behind a note and a pigeon at the scene of the crime, promising to return the car if the owner puts cash into a container on the homing pigeon's leg.

'We have tried to catch the thieves by using telescopes to follow the birds,' said a police spokesman, 'but they flew too high and too fast and we lost sight of them.'

A delinquent duck also made off with a gold watch belonging to pub landlord Raymond Charman. The duck swallowed the £500 watch when Mr Charman took if off to wash his car in Corby, Northamptonshire. A furious chase ensued with the duck finally taking to the air and flying away.

In 1969, the chickens on a French farm became so depressed that they almost stopped laying eggs altogether. A top French animal psychiatrist was called in. After much consideration, he pronounced that the chickens were madly jealous of the doves flying above the farm. The chickens could see them but couldn't fly themselves. His solution was to suspend each chicken from balloons for two hours every day so that they too might experience the wonders of flight. Apparently, this therapy worked and the chickens went back to laying eggs as usual.

Donald the duck was the mascot of the 2nd Gordon Highlanders during the Second World War. She was captured by the Japanese and would have been killed, except for an extraordinary bluff by a quick-thinking Scottish corporal, William Gray. He convinced his Japanese captors that the Scots were a race of heathen duck-worshippers! Donald was very sacred, he told them, and needed to be worshipped every single morning at sunrise by the entire company. The superstitious Japanese guards withdrew their death threat and trod very warily around Donald from then on. Donald, for her part, went on to regularly lay eggs for the hungry prisoners of war, and survived to return to Scotland with Corporal Gray.

The bird man of Alcatraz was a convicted double murderer, Robert Franklin Stroud, sentenced to spend his entire life in solitary confinement. He started out by adopting two sparrows who came to visit him in his cell, and discovered he had a strong affinity for birds. The authorities encouraged his hobby, giving him a spare cell and the equipment he needed. Stroud went on to become a world famous expert, writing a famous book on bird diseases and selling medicines and birds which he'd bred himself. His most famous customer was J Edgar Hoover, head of the FBI!

Joko the parrot pleaded the fifth amendment – the right to stay silent on the grounds that he might incriminate himself – when he went up before the beak in an Oslo courtroom charged with being a major source of noise pollution.

800,000 racing pigeons were called up for service with the British Armed Forces during the Second World War. So important was their work, carrying top-secret messages, that a squadron of Nazi hawks were stationed near Paris to intercept the birds. 31 pigeons won Dickin Medals for gallantry during the war – more than any other type of animal.

Today, the Swiss Army has some 40,000 carrier pigeons on its payroll. The pigeons now carry information on microchips rather than on a note. This means that whole volumes of books can be carried by just one pigeon on a single flight.

Incidentally, homing pigeons were being used as early as 1150 BC, by the Sultan of Baghdad.

The Allied HQ on the Western Front raced to decipher the message that had just been delivered from the trenches by a carrier pigeon. It read, simply, 'Lucky pigeon to get out of this hell of a place!'

One bird saved a thousand lives during the Second World War and was awarded a chest full of medals, including a medal for gallantry, by the Lord Mayor of London, as well as a Congressional Honour in the USA. He was also the first non-British animal to receive the Dickin Medal for bravery.

The bird was a homing pigeon named GI Joe who was based in Italy. The British 56th Infantry Division was trying to break the German defensive lines in the fortified village of Colvi Vecchia. A major push was going to take place on 18 October, 1943, and the British requested air support. However, just after this had been confirmed, the ground troops made a surprise breakthrough and managed to route the German resistance, enabling them to take over the town. There was now no need for air support, but as they tried to cancel their request, British troops made the chilling discovery that, in the advance, the radio equipment had been damaged. Unless they could get word to cancel the air support they would end up being bombed by their own aircraft! There was only one hope – a homing pigeon just might make it back in time. GI Joe was chosen to undertake this critical mission.

GI Joe took off and flew the twenty hazardous miles over war-torn countryside in just twenty minutes, achieving an average of 60mph. Just as he landed, the Allied Air Support planes were preparing to take off and were taxiing down the runway. His message was relayed to the base commander and the mission was cancelled in time. If it hadn't been for a little speckled pigeon called GI Joe, over 1,000 Allied soldiers could have been killed by their own bombers.

After the war, GI Joe retired to the USA, living in comfort at the Army's Churchill Lofts – special accommodation built just for pigeons who'd served over twenty combat missions. GI Joe spent his last days at Detroit Zoo where he became a star attraction until his death in 1961.

The United States Army first started using homing pigeons during the Sioux uprising of 1878. This tradition has continued, reaching its peak during the Second World War when an estimated 56,000 birds were in service, with an extremely high rate of success.

The Romanian tyrant Nicolae Ceauşescu owned a parrot which lived in absolute luxury while his servants were beaten and bullied. As revenge, the servants decided they would try to teach the parrot to chant anti-Ceauşescu propaganda. Nothing happened until one day when the president held a top-level meeting with all his military chiefs of staff. Everyone had assembled and talks had just begun when the parrot, perched in the corner started flapping around his cage making rude noises and screeching, 'Stupid Nico! Stupid Nico!' There was a stunned silence – except of course for the parrot, who kept on abusing the red-faced president. The military men knew they dare not laugh at any price and had to keep their giggles restrained as the parrot kept on taunting Ceauşescu and the president unwisely started yelling insults back at the parrot.

The next day, the parrot was gone, and was never mentioned again…

It sounded as if the quiet market town of Gulsborough, Cleveland, was in the grip of a major crimewave. People all over the town were being woken up at first light by the loud shrill sound of car alarms going off. Rushing outside in their nightclothes, they found their cars untouched. The police were baffled until a local journalist, Mark Topping, became a victim of the phantom car alarm and spotted the real culprit. 'At first, it seemed to be a car alarm, but there wasn't one close enough to be making that sort of row,' he said. 'Then I saw this blackbird in the tree right outside the bedroom window! I was amazed. It could hardly have chosen a more irritating thing to mimic!'

David Hirst of the RSPB suggested that one blackbird could have taught the new 'song' it had learned to others in the area, which is why the entire town was plagued by early morning alarm calls. 'It is quite extraordinary,' he said. 'Starlings are normally the Rory Bremners of the bird world!'

The bird that's recorded as covering the greatest distance migrating is an Arctic tern. It was ringed in Russia in 1955 and captured alive by a fisherman in Western Australia later that year. The bird had travelled a staggering 14,000 miles.

The Arctic tern makes a regular annual journey between breeding seasons from the North Pole to the South Pole – then back again. After that sort of trip, you'd wonder where he found the energy to breed.

Jenny the budgie, who belonged to June Lowton of Nottingham, could do a very convincing impression – of a dead budgie.

Unlike all other budgies, Jenny refused to sleep on her perch with her head tucked under her wing. Instead she would lie flat on the floor of her cage with her feet stuck in the air.

Racing pigeons are, and were, owned by some of the most diverse people in the world, including Yul Brynner, boxer Marvin Hagler, the King of Thailand and, of course, our Queen.

Pigeon racing is the national sport of Belgium and was introduced to the UK in 1871. The largest racing pigeon stud is near Loughborough, Leicestershire – about twenty years ago, the owner paid £77,000 for a Dutch bird named Emerald (a fellow pigeon fancier paid £2,400 for her first egg, before it had even hatched!).

In 1896 the Tass news agency in Moscow reported that a Russian parrot could recite Shakespeare's eighth sonnet in English and could also give an accurate rendition of a Pushkin poem (apparently, it preferred the English translation). The bird's owner was Boris Kozyrev from Minsk, who's said to be a fan of English language lessons on Russian TV.

A parrot escaped from its cage in Healdsburg, California, in October 1986 and rested at the top of a tall tree. According to the *Sun* newspaper, it taunted firemen who tried to rescue it by shouting down at them, 'I can talk. Can you fly?'

Two ducks on a farm in Dyfed in Wales started laying black eggs on St David's Day (1 March) 1986. By May they had laid a total of thirty-six of them, ranging from dark grey to pitch black – no one could explain why.

A woodpecker hammers its beak at an amazing 15 times a second, nearly twice the speed of a machine gun. At this rate its head reaches a speed of up to 1,300mph. To avoid concussion, its beak and brain are extremely well cushioned.

*Chapter Nine*

# BRAVEST OF THE BRAVE

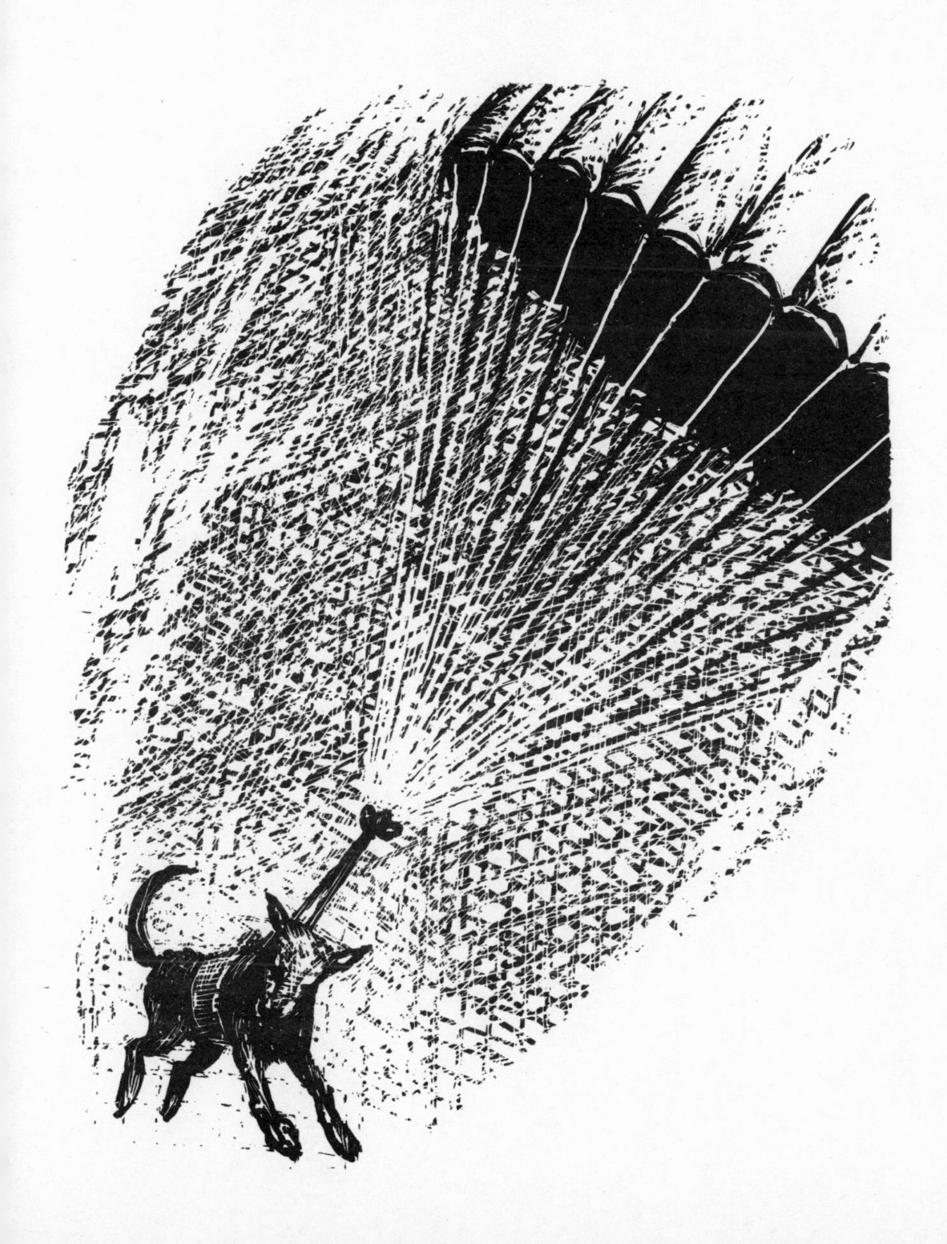

Max was a 90lb rust-coloured boxer and the mascot of the US 505th Parachute Infantry. In 1942 the regiment was stationed at Fort Benning in Georgia and Max was desperate to go up with his colleagues on training flights. He would trot alongside them as they marched up to the aircraft and would bark loudly as the plane taxied and eventually took off – without him.

Eventually though, they gave in to his demands and rigged Max out with a special parachute and harness attached to a static line.

On his first flight, Max was going to be second out of the plane after Jump Master Lt Clyde Russell. The door was opened and Max stuck his wet nose out into the air rushing by. Lt Russell jumped – and so did Max, without any hesitation. His 22-foot chute opened and Max slowly glided to earth, keeping the correct distance from the other jumpers as he descended. He landed feet first – which was better than most human novices – and calmly waited where he landed for the other jumpers to get to him and remove his harness.

It takes five jumps to qualify as a parachutist and Max was a bit more nervous the second time. He jumped perfectly though – with a stunning four-point landing. The next three jumps were fine and after his fifth jump, a review was held in his honour. Max was presented with his silver wings by Colonel

James McGavin, the regiment's commanding officer, and his fame spread. In jumping, Max not only demonstrated his own bravery, but gave courage and encouragement to some of the more nervous human recruits at the base.

But it's not just American dogs that make fearless parachutists. War Dog No 471/322, better known as Rob, a collie cross, served with the SAS in North Africa, as their official 'Paradog'. He took part in infantry landings and parachuted into enemy territory with advanced exploration parties, working closely with raiding parties that operated behind enemy lines, sabotaging their gun emplacements and munitions supplies. On many occasions, Rob was able to save the lives of his masters by giving them warning of approaching Italian or German patrols. He was fitted out with a specially designed harness and made over twenty parachute jumps behind enemy lines, never showing any fear.

Rob survived the war and was presented with the Dickin Medal in 1945, the animal kingdom's equivalent of the Victoria Cross.

Brian, an Alsatian cross, served in the British 13th Battalion Airborne Division. He was landed in Normandy and carried out enough drops to become a qualified parachutist, saving many lives in his distinguished career. He was also awarded a Dickin Medal for his exceptional courage.

Scarlett must be just about the bravest cat in the whole of America – and the proudest mum. When the garage which she called home caught fire with her kittens still inside, the plucky tortoiseshell stray didn't hesitate. Five times she raced into the inferno, each time emerging with a precious little bundle gripped safely in her jaws. She set each four-week-old kitten down on the kerb across the street and dashed back for the next. By the time she'd rescued them all, the smoke was so bad she could hardly see – so she counted her kittens up by touching them in turn with her nose. Satisfied that all five were safe, she then let rescuers take the family off to a local animal shelter for treatment.

Scarlett and her family all recovered and her bravery made headline news around the world. In fact, the animal sanctuary in Brooklyn, New York, received over 1,000 calls – some from as far away as Canada and London – from people wanting to offer Scarlett and her family a good home. Marge Stern, manager of the North Shore Animal League shelter, wasn't surprised. 'She's a wonderful animal who did a courageous thing,' she said. 'Even with animals, there's no way of measuring a mother's love.'

Mourka the tom cat ran urgent errands for the Soviet Army during the Siege of Stalingrad in the Second World War. Stationed with an artillery detachment, he would have a message attached to his collar and then run the gauntlet of fire to the local Russian headquarters. Once there, he would be fed and looked after and sent back to his comrades after a good night's rest.

Simon was the black and white ship's cat on board HMS *Amethyst* and the personal pet of her commanding officer, Lt Cmdr I R Griffiths. The warship was trapped in the Yangtse River by Red Chinese forces in 1949, and shelled mercilessly. Simon survived an almost direct hit and went on to become a symbol of inspiration for the ship's crew in the months they were besieged before the ship finally broke out and escaped to Hong Kong. He was mentioned in despatches to London for his devotion to duty under fire and recommended for a medal.

Simon became a household name around the world. He had his own fan club and was showered with gifts from well-wishers, including of course tins of fish and cans of cream, as well as gaily coloured ribbons. For his heroism and his part in keeping up the morale of the ship's crew, Simon was awarded the Dickin Medal. He is the only cat ever to have won this award.

His little tombstone, at the PDSA cemetery in Ilford, Essex, bears HMS *Amethyst*'s emblem as well as a fitting inscription:

Now here's Simon
For me to make a rhyme on,
Gallant little Simon,
The Amethyst's cat.
Proper Royal Navy!
Give him all the gravy,
He's not daunted
By the slowest rat.

It's not often that a cat gets a chance to be a have-a-go hero, but that's exactly what happened to plucky Lucky in the small village of Abbot's Moreton in Worcestershire.

Lucky belonged to the owner of the sub-post office there and when it was held up by an armed raider, she leaped over the counter and stuck her claws into the gunman, making him shriek and then flee in terror!

She was rewarded with a new blue silk cushion and a medal from the Postmaster General.

Mustapha was a dog who served at the Battle of Fontenoy in 1745. The gun crew he was with were all killed or injured and about to be overrun by the enemy. The cannon had been loaded but there was no one to fire it. Mustapha had watched the crew in action time after time so he knew what had to be done. Although wounded himself, he took hold of the lighted torch in his mouth and lit the fuse. The cannon roared one final time, and when the smoke cleared, 70 advancing French soldiers were no more.

A very brave bird was the homing pigeon, Cher Ami. He was attached to an American infantry unit in France in the First World War and served with distinction, delivering many important messages. His most important mission, however, was his last and took place on 4 October, 1918.

In the early days of that month, Cher Ami's unit had suffered heavy casualties under intense German artillery fire and they desperately needed reinforcements. The only way to send for help was via homing pigeon and an urgent communication was attached to Cher Ami. He took off for the divisional headquarters, but, as he gained height, he was shot by a German sniper and plummeted to the ground. After flapping around in confusion, Cher Ami took off once more – but seconds later he was hit again. Ignoring any pain Cher Ami once more took off, but was hit again – and again, in the breastbone and leg. Some inner force drove Cher Ami on and he struggled the twenty miles to headquarters, the plea for help still attached to his damaged body. The SOS was read and reinforcements immediately dispatched, saving the lives of many of the soldiers under fire.

Miraculously, Cher Ami survived his injuries and was awarded the Croix de Guerre, one of the highest awards presented in France for gallantry in wartime. He returned to the US after the war where he died peacefully in 1919, a national hero. Cher Ami's body was mounted and put on display in Washington's Smithsonian Institute.

The novelist Sir Walter Scott's dog, Maida, lived with him at his home, Forbes Castle. In 1825 a fire broke out while Scott was fast asleep. He awoke coughing and spluttering, his bedroom full of thick, acrid smoke. Completely disoriented and fighting for breath, he was about to pass out when Maida grabbed him by his night clothes. She dragged him out of bed and into the laundry room to safety.

Brett was an Alsatian who was trained as a guard dog, and who won over a dozen awards for bravery in his long career. His first award came from the RSPCA for rescuing two terriers that had fallen down a mine shaft in Yorkshire (it took Brett six dangerous attempts to reach them, but he refused to give up!).

On other occasions he rescued sheep from large snowdrifts and a young girl from drowning by grabbing her swimming costume lightly in his teeth and pulling her out of danger. Once Brett rescued a kitten that was adrift on a log in a river by tenderly lifting the kitten from the log with his mouth and holding her there while he swam to the shore.

Brett also had the distinction of successfully tackling thieves and was the first guard dog to leap from a helicopter while chasing a criminal.

Brett died aged fourteen in 1974 after a distinguished career and is buried in the middle of Snowdonia. A simple grave with an even simpler inscription sums up Brett's celebrated life: 'He Mastered Them All'.

In the winter of 1983 Ian Elliot was cutting down trees on his Canadian farm when a massive pine tree crashed down on him. The impact broke his back and trapped him in a shallow, but icy, river. No one was around apart from his faithful sheepdog, Braken.

Braken sensed what to do and immediately lay down on top of Ian to maintain his body temperature. His thick coat kept Ian alive and after three hours he heard the distant voices of some other men. Braken raced off and chased the voices for over a mile until he came across a party of lumberjacks. By barking he managed to persuade them to follow him back to where Ian lay in the river. Ian was rushed to a nearby hospital where staff praised the actions of Braken. Without his quick thinking, Ian would have certainly died from exposure.

When the Spanish explorer Hernando Cortez travelled from Cuba to Mexico in 1519, he took with him sixteen horses. His favourite was a fine black stallion called Morzillo, who one day saved his life.

In one battle, Cortez was pulled off his horse by Indian warriors. He struggled on the ground to avoid capture, but was eventually saved by Morzillo, who charged at the Indians, pounding at them with his flailing hooves until help arrived.

In 1524, Cortez was on an expedition in Honduras when Morzillo became lame with a large splinter in one of his hooves. Cortez was forced to leave him with Mayan Indians, who had never seen a horse before. At first they had thought that Cortez and his horse were a single, great beast – a sort of centaur. They regarded Morzillo as a deity and worshipped him as Tziminchac, 'God of Thunder', bringing him gifts of gold, covering him with garlands of flowers and sweet-smelling incense. They even built a life-size black stone statue of him, which they worshipped after

Morzillo's eventual death. This statue was destroyed as an idol years later by Spanish missionaries. However, today in the region, the legend of Morzillo, the Horse-God lives on.

In July 1985, Liu Ming-hui, a Taiwanese farmer, was travelling with his prize pig when they were involved in a road accident. Liu was badly injured but his pig was untouched. The pig scuttled off to fetch help and soon returned to the deserted stretch of road where Liu was lying with rescuers close behind.

Stig was the dog that nobody wanted. A big, boisterous Alsatian, he was getting too large for the Rongemo family's flat in Malmo, Sweden. Worse, the Rongemos didn't want him around their two-year-old daughter, Mariette. Although they regarded the dog as soppy and a bit 'thick', they were worried that he might accidentally hurt her. There was only one thing for it. Stig had to go. The trouble was, no one wanted him. Then, while the family were still trying to work out what to do with him, something truly extraordinary happened. Lief Rongemo walked into his bedroom, straight into a scene from his worst nightmares. His little daughter Mariette had toddled out of an open window and was now crawling along a perilous narrow ledge outside their tower block home – over ninety feet above the pavement. As Lief stared at the scene in horror, he realised that Stig the Alsatian had followed Mariette out onto the ledge and was now inching up behind her...

Lief screamed for his wife to phone the fire brigade and rushed down into the street. He and a passer-by held a blanket out under the ledge, in the desperate hope that they might be able to catch the little girl if she fell.

Stig, meanwhile, had caught up with Mariette. His powerful jaws clamped around the toddler's britches and, with the child firmly in his grip, he started to edge his way backwards along the ledge again. It seemed to take for ever, but eventually Stig got the toddler back to the open window and the mother pulled them both inside.

'We owe Stig more than we can ever repay,' Leif said later. 'From now on, it's only the best steak money can buy for him!'

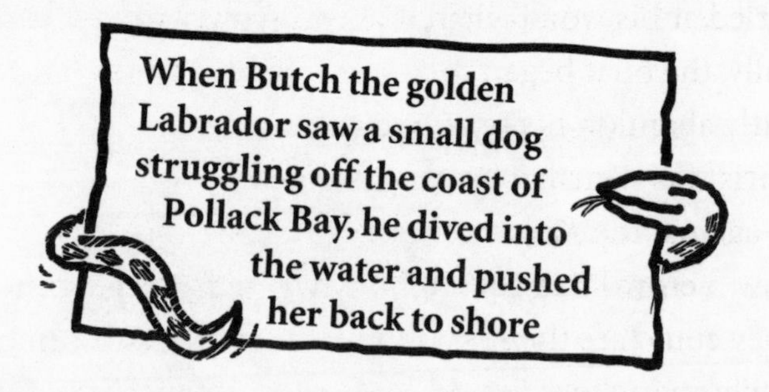

This next tale is about a brave dog – but also an equally brave would-be rescuer…

It was a treacherous December night as the trawler *Kergal* battled a heavy storm to make her way home to France. She was just off the Cornish coast when a huge wave appeared from nowhere, swamping the boat and flooding its engines. The coastguard received the captain's SOS within minutes, but the strength of the storm made it impossible to launch the nearby Penlee lifeboat. For the first time in its long service, waves had actually swept it off the slipway. The only way to get assistance to the trawler was by the Royal Navy, and three air-sea rescue helicopters took off from the Culdrose Naval Base. In the meantime the trawler had been blown onto rocks and was taking in water faster than it could be pumped out.

Force 9 gales made it almost impossible to manoeuvre a

helicopter safely near to the trawler, but one eventually managed to winch down a crewman, Leading Seaman Chris Burrows, who lifted in turn each of the trawler's five-man crew to safety.

It was only as the last man was rescued that Chris learned there was another crew member aboard – the trawler's dog, a cross bred spaniel called Mousse who had been aboard the *Kergal* since he was a puppy.

Risking his life for another descent, Chris Burrows landed on board the stricken trawler and tried to coax Mousse out of the wheelhouse where he was hiding. Mousse was obviously terrified and snarled at his would-be rescuer whenever Chris came near. Eventually, the boat began to break up and Chris had to reluctantly abandon his rescue attempt.

As Chris was winched back up to his helicopter, a huge wave crashed against the *Kergal*, sweeping Mousse into the sea.

By now, a crowd had gathered on the beach and in the search-lights they could see the spaniel struggling in the cresting waves, desperately trying to swim ashore. Risking their own safety, six of the strongest men tied themselves together and waded into the sea as far as they dared, to make it easier for Mousse to reach safety. Twice Mousse almost came within their reach – only to be swept away at the last moment.

By now he was finding it difficult holding his head above water and his strength was flagging. The men shouted encouragement and, mustering every ounce of energy in his weary little body, Mousse surged forward against the tide. This time one of the men managed to grab him and hold onto him as waves battered them both. The human chain pulled them ashore. Mousse was wet, terrified and covered in oil from the trawler's wreckage. He was rushed to an animal hospital in Penzance and cared for by the RSPCA. A few days later he had made a full recovery and sailed back to France on another trawler, to be reunited with his old crew.

Chris Burrows is often asked why he risked his life to save Mousse when he'd done enough by saving the five crewmen. He unselfishly replies, 'I'm an animal lover and I felt I had to make the attempt.'

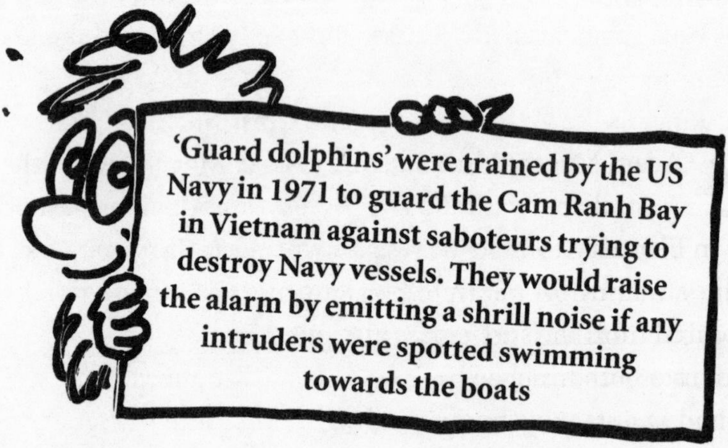

**'Guard dolphins' were trained by the US Navy in 1971 to guard the Cam Ranh Bay in Vietnam against saboteurs trying to destroy Navy vessels. They would raise the alarm by emitting a shrill noise if any intruders were spotted swimming towards the boats**

While he was growing up, the mighty Spanish warrior, El Cid, was offered a choice of horses by his godfather. After observing them for several days he chose the poorest looking foal – a thin white, awkward-looking colt. His godfather thought that El Cid had made a very bad choice and named the horse 'Babieca', which meant 'a fool'. But El Cid trained him well and proved his godfather wrong. El Cid became leader of the Spanish forces and Babieca carried him to victory after victory against the Moors.

In his last great battle, El Cid was mortally wounded and on his death bed he requested that he be secretly embalmed and carried into battle on Babieca one last time. His wish was honoured and El Cid was prepared and dressed in his finest armour, then mounted in the saddle of loyal Babieca. On the battlefield, El Cid's forces were outnumbered and demoralised. The fighting was going against them, when Babieca burst through their lines carrying El Cid. Inspired by his appearance (they had thought him dead), the Spanish troops rallied and defeated the Moors.

El Cid was buried after the battle and Babieca lived for two more years before being buried with dignity at a monastery in Castile.

Adam Maguire, like most average seventeen-year-old Australians, was mad keen on surfing. One hot summer's day in February 1989 he was surfing off the north coast of Sydney, waiting for a wave, when a thirteen-foot shark suddenly appeared from the surf, smashing into Adam and sinking its teeth into both his board and his side. Adam began splashing around in a state of shock, having lost quite a lot of blood. By now the shark was moving in for the kill, but was spotted by a nearby school of dolphins.

They thrashed wildly about in the water around the shark, distracting it. Then they swam in circles around it, giving Adam's friends a chance to pull him to safety. By the time they got him to the shore, the shark had swum back out to sea. Adam was rushed to hospital for emergency surgery and a blood transfusion and survived to tell his story – owing his life to the brave efforts of the intelligent dolphins.

An accident on Ansty Farm in Sussex in April 1985 soon had the entire barn in flames, trapping most of the sheep and cattle inside. The blaze was so intense that farm workers had to abandon their attempts to save the trapped animals. Just when it looked as if they would all perish, Nipper, the farm's five-year-old collie came to the rescue.

He braved the heat and the smoke time and time again to shepherd frightened calves and lambs to safety. He even managed to lead some of the much bigger sheep and cows out, and by his efforts almost all the animals survived. Nipper escaped with singed fur and blistered paws, and was awarded the Dickin Medal engraved with a dedication for his 'intelligence and courage'.

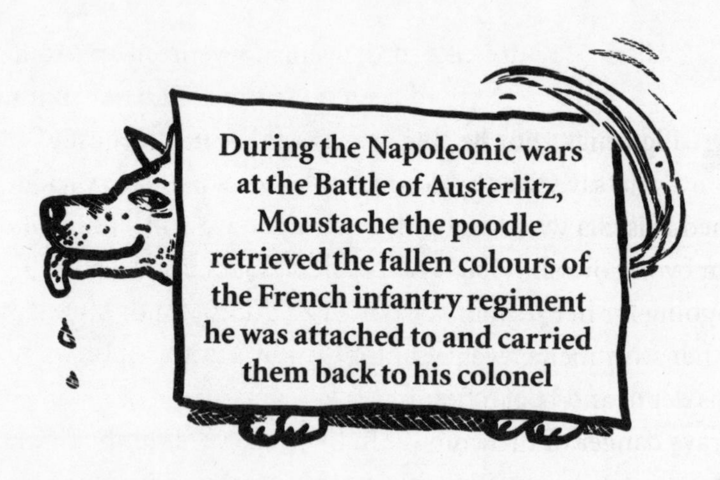


A cat named Lizzie was the mascot on board an American trawler, the *Whitecap*. While she was at sea a fire broke out in the galley and soon most of the boat was alight. Smoke was billowing into the cabin where Gus Dunsky, the trawler's captain, was fast asleep. Despite the danger, Lizzie jumped through the smoke and flames and frantically clawed at Gus with her paws until she woke him, saving his life.

Robert Moodie was fishing with his nine-year-old dog at an estuary near Cairns in Northern Queensland in March 1996 when he dropped one of his lures into the murky water. Resting his rods on the bank, he dived in to retrieve it, only to be hit and almost knocked unconscious by a gigantic crocodile. Seeing his master in danger, Robert's dog jumped in and managed to chase the crocodile away before dragging his owner safely back to the river bank.

Mr Moodie was in shock, but recovered. He owes his life to his dog – a creature that proved conclusively that he didn't deserve his unfortunate name – Stupid.

Pigs might not be able to fly, but they can certainly swim – and save lives by doing so. That was proved by a pig named Priscilla who lived in Houston and who was taught to swim by her owner, Victoria Herberta. On 29 July 1984, Priscilla was going for her regular paddle in Lake Somerville when another swimmer, eleven-year-old Anthony Melton, strayed out of his depth and began floundering in the middle of the lake – in grave danger of drowning.

Hearing his cries for help, Priscilla swam straight towards Anthony, who was by now in great difficulty. She managed to reach the boy and, using her snout, kept his head above water until he could get a firm grip on her collar. Then, with trotters thrashing, she managed to swim to the shore, dragging him to safety.

Priscilla became Houston's hero and was awarded the 1984 William O Stillman Award, given annually by the American Humane Society to animals who save human lives. But her greatest day came on 25 August the same year, when the Mayor of Houston proclaimed that the day was to be 'Priscilla the Pig Day' in honour of one of the state's bravest citizens!

*Chapter Ten*

# Celebrity Animals

Pringle the penguin, star of the *Russell Harty Show*, was a bit of a loony right from the word go. First off, he hated water – somewhat of a problem if you're a king penguin. Secondly, he hated other penguins. What Pringle liked was people. He'd spend all day at the edge of his enclosure in Chessington World of Adventure 'talking' to the visitors and shunning his fellow birds. Pringle's keeper, Ron Eaton, became convinced that Pringle thought he was human. The huge bird refused to travel to the TV studio in a regular penguin crate – but would quite happily waddle onto the back seat of a chauffeur-driven car and travel there in style.

'Trigger' was the stage name of a beautiful golden palomino which was originally named Golden Cloud – and the star of no less than 87 films!

His regular co-star, Roy Rogers, was under no illusions as to why people flocked to see his movies. 'Just as many fans are interested in seeing Trigger as they are in seeing me,' he admitted.

Although he will always be associated with Roy Rogers, Trigger actually made his screen debut in 1938 alongside another star, Errol Flynn, in *The Adventures of Robin Hood*. His thirty-year association with Roy began shortly after that and continued into the late 1950s on the popular TV series *The Roy Rogers Show With Dale Evans.*

Trigger was an exceptionally intelligent horse and knew over 60 tricks, including signing his name (an 'X') by holding a pen in his teeth, walking 150 yards on his hind legs, drinking milk from a bottle, taking a gun out of a holster with his mouth and doing simple addition or subtraction, as well as counting up to twenty (by stomping his hooves, of course). Rogers called Trigger 'the smartest horse in the movies' – and he was.

Probably the most famous elephant in the movies was Anna May. At the peak of her success she literally was the biggest thing in films. Anna May was the natural choice to play Jumbo, in *The Mighty Barnum*, the story of P T Barnum and his circus. The only problem was that she was an Indian elephant, and Jumbo was a huge African beast. But, at times like these the studio make-up department can usually be relied upon to save the day – and they did. They made a huge pair of false ears and a pair of false tusks that fitted over her smaller ones.

Anna May appeared in many Tarzan films, alongside Douglas Fairbanks in *The Lives of a Bengal Lancer,* and in Charlie Chaplin's *City Lights.*

Being a particularly bright elephant, Anna May would not tolerate anyone smoking on the set of her films. If she spotted someone pulling out a pack, she would flick out her trunk, confiscate the cigarettes – and chew them up!

Jimmy the raven starred in James Stewart's Oscar-winning movie *You Can't Take It With You* and appeared in more than 200 other films. Jimmy often stole the show from his human co-stars with an amazing array of tricks. These included straightening an actor's tie and pocket handkerchief, playing cards, stealing money and jewels, lighting cigarettes and opening locks. He could even type a letter and operate a cash register.

I only know of one oyster with special talents, and that was Molly the Whistling Oyster. As you might guess, this oyster had musical skills, previously unknown among shellfish.

Molly was discovered by a shopkeeper called Pearkes in 1840. She was one of a cask of oysters in his shop in Drury Lane, London. A high-pitched warble was heard coming from the cask and Pearkes held each oyster up to his ear in turn until he discovered that the sound was coming from Molly. She was put on display at his shop as a curiosity and soon actors from the nearby Theatre Royal and visitors all around flocked to his shop to be serenaded by the musical mollusc.

Molly was soon the toast of London and Pearkes turned down large sums of money from circus owners and theatre managers to buy her. A music artist of the time, Sam Cowell, wrote a song about her, drawings appeared in *Punch* – which called her 'a phenomenal bivalve' – and soon everyone was gossiping or joking about her. One jealous American visitor told the novelist Thackeray that in Massachusetts there is an oyster, 'that whistles "Yankee Doodle" – and even follows its master around the house like a dog.'

Molly flourished for a long time in a tub of brine, enchanting visitors day by day, but few, if any, enquired about how an oyster could sing.

In fact, the secret of Molly's extraordinary talent was a small defect in her shell; water was expelled through this pinhole as Molly 'breathed' – and that was what made the haunting whistling sound.

All the odds were definitely against Red Rum, but, just as on the track, he came through to become the most celebrated race horse of all time.

He was bred for flat racing instead of the jumps, and his mother developed a mental condition which vets feared might be hereditary. People kept buying and selling him, with no real enthusiasm for his future.

When he was bought for 6,000 guineas at Doncaster Sales in 1972 by trainer Ginger McCain, he was already seven years old and stricken with pedalostitis, a bone-wasting disease which is usually incurable. Despite this, McCain stuck with his first impression – that there was something special about Rummy – and he was right.

Red Rum went on to win the Grand National three times and come second twice more, gaining himself a place in the hearts of people everywhere. After retiring, he earned six-figure sums for putting in personal appearances at shows and supermarket openings and for the rest of his days stayed with the trainer – the one man who had faith in him when no one else did.

Sparkie was a budgie with an insatiable appetite for words. He was bought in 1954 by Mattie Williams, an English teacher from Newcastle-upon-Tyne. She had never owned a bird before, but in a few days had taught him to say 'Pretty Sparkie'. After this Sparkie learned new words every day. His vocabulary included words he'd been taught by Mattie and those which he'd overheard.

Nine months later, Sparkie knew over 300 words. He was entered in a national talking budgie competition organised by the BBC and he beat nearly 2,800 rivals to take the first prize. Building on this success, Sparkie made a number of TV commercials for bird seed under the stage name 'Mr Chatterbox' and even made a record that taught owners how to teach their budgies to talk. By the end of his career, Sparkie had mastered 531 words, 383 sentences and 8 nursery rhymes. He died aged eight, in 1962, in the hands of his beloved owner Mattie Williams and his last words were 'I love you mamma'.

In 1989, the Belgian director Armando Acosta made a version of *Romeo and Juliet* – with an all-stray-cat cast! Juliet was played by a cloud-white long-haired Turkish angora, whom the director described as 'the Marilyn Monroe of the cat world', while the role of Romeo went to a bear-furred grey, found close to death and nursed back to health by Armando and a team of vets.

'I directed them like people,' he said. 'By watching I knew how they would behave.' Despite this, 200 hours of footage had to be shot before the film was finished. After the end-of-shooting party, new homes were found for the entire cast – except for Romeo and Juliet. Armando couldn't bear to part with them and they went to live with him in Ghent in Belgium.

In April 1996, Battersea Dogs' Home received one of their strangest ever requests – for a dog that looked like actress Zoë Wanamaker! The dog was needed to star in a new West End comedy called *Sylvia*. Zoë personally inspected the ten dogs that the home put on audition for her, all of which allegedly bore a passing resemblance to the comedy actress. She couldn't decide between Katie with her 'sweet little face and tufty coat' and Whisky, an unashamed scruff with a great personality, so director Michael Blakemore was called in for the casting vote. He chose three-year-old Katie.

Katie's adopted owner, Pauline Gayle, says, 'she's a fantastic dog and loves everyone – but she's a bit greedy and fat. She certainly loves all the attention she's getting at the moment!'

Battersea said they were delighted that one of their 'old girls' had been chosen for stardom, as she helped to make people think about the plight of strays. Zoë too, was enchanted by her canine co-star. 'Katie has an upturned nose and lots of hair on top, a bit like mine,' she says, 'but I'm not really sure about the moustache!'

A tiny black kitten turned up on the steps of 10 Downing Street on the day Winston Churchill addressed the Conservative Party at their annual conference in 1953. This conference was vital to Churchill's political career, since he had had two strokes and people were questioning whether he was capable of leading his party. However, his speeches were a great success and he saw the black cat as a good omen, choosing to name her after the conference venue – Margate.

Alexander the Great, King of Macedonia in the 4th century BC, kept two loyal and trusted animals – a pointer named Pepitas and a white charger called Bucephalus. They accompanied Alexander everywhere he went, even to his famous victories in Greece, Persia and Egypt. Buchephalus was a wild horse which Alexander trained – legend has it that he would let no one except Alexander ride him. He lived to be thirty years of age and in the course of eight and a half years, travelled over 11,000 miles.

When Pepitas died he was given a full state funeral as a national hero. In honour of Bucephalus, Alexander founded a city – on the spot where the horse had died in 327 BC – calling it Bucephala.

The Roman poet Virgil (70–19 BC) had a favourite pet – a housefly. When it died, he held a lavish funeral ceremony in the grounds of his huge mansion on the Esquiline Hill in Rome. Virgil hired human mourners to pay their last respects to the fly – which was buried in a special mausoleum to the accompaniment of an orchestra. His patron, Maecenas, gave a long and moving speech and Virgil ended the proceedings by reading some poetry he'd composed especially for the occasion.

It is estimated that the whole ceremony cost in excess of £50,000. Why? Of course, it's possible that Virgil was a bit mad, but it's more likely the cunning old so-and-so did it all as an elaborate tax dodge! The Roman rulers of the day were planning to confiscate some of his land – but made an exception for any ground which had been used as a burial plot.

Coco the talkative parrot belonged to Prince Leopold of Belgium and sang duets with his wife Charlotte, George IV's daughter. Coco was so affected by her death in 1817, that he never sang again.

Blackbird was the fierce chief of the Omaha Indians who spent most of his time in the saddle. He loved horses so much that he instructed his braves to bury him still sitting on the back of his favourite mount – which they duly did.

Incitatus means 'fast speeding' and was the name of the horse belonging to the Roman Emperor Caligula (37–71 AD). However, Incitatus started life with a much less noble name – Porcellus (the little pig).

The much grander name was bestowed on him when Caligula first realised just how fast he could run. From that day, Incitatus became his favourite horse – and never lost a race. To show his gratitude for the victories of Incitatus, Caligula treated him as he would visiting royalty, even giving him his own villa. Incitatus was attended by an entourage of slaves. He slept in sweet-smelling straw (that was changed each day) in the middle of a huge marble bedroom. The manger was made of ivory and the drinking trough was solid gold. To make sure Incitatus wasn't wakened, he used to send soldiers through the town, ordering the locals to keep quiet.

Further honours came when Caligula first made Incitatus a citizen of Rome, then a senator. It's said that Caligula was even considering making his race horse a Consul – one of the two elected magistrates who had the highest authority in Rome.

Incitatus was always invited to the wild parties Caligula would throw on a whim, eating whatever the other guests were having. On one occasion he accidentally smashed into an ornamental cup that had belonged to Julius Caesar. Caligula was very superstitious and thought this was a bad omen. It may well have been – Caligula was assassinated not long afterwards.

*Chapter Eleven*

# LIFE-SAVERS

A family of wolves in Azerbaijan immediately adopted a little three-year-old girl, Mekhriban Ibagimov, when she got lost in the woods. Rescuers found her safe and sound, snuggled up to a big she-wolf and her three cubs. 'A big wolf licked my face,' she recalle. 'I snuggled up and she kept me warm. The little puppies cried'.

Gilbert the goose lived on the farm belonging to Edgar Ormiston in Otterburn, Northumberland. Gilbert had lost his mate in 1984, but soon found a new friend in a pregnant ewe. The two quickly became inseparable, but then, a few weeks later, the ewe suddenly collapsed right in front of her feathered friend.

Gilbert tugged at her fleece with his beak in an effort to get her up. This didn't work so he ran round the farm, flapping his wings and honking loudly until he'd attracted Edgar's attention. The farmer came running, took one look at the ewe and called the vet. Thanks to Gilbert's prompt action, both the ewe and her lamb survived.

Ray Ellis was cutting firewood with a chainsaw, accompanied by his German shepherd called Girl. While he was sawing, a heavy branch fell and knocked Ray unconscious. As he collapsed, his chainsaw also fell and severely injured his foot. Girl saw this and immediately ran a quarter of a mile home to raise the alarm. Pounding on the front door with her paws, Girl alerted Ray's wife, Dorothy. The dog's frantic whining and yelping immediately convinced Dorothy that something was wrong and she ran after Girl into the woods. There she saw Ray lying still on the ground. He'd lost a lot of blood so she dashed back home again to call for an ambulance. While Dorothy did this, Girl stayed by her master's side, licking his face until medical help came.

Thanks to Girl's quick thinking, Ray is now on the road to a full recovery. While recuperating in hospital he couldn't express enough thanks to his trusty pet, telling reporters, 'I wouldn't be here if not for Girl. I'm the luckiest man alive to have a friend like her.'

When Sir Henry Wyatt was flung into the Tower of London in 1483 and left to starve or freeze to death in a damp, cold cell, his jailers thought he had only weeks to live at best. But Sir Henry confounded them and survived, eventually to be released – and he owed it all to a stray cat. The stray had befriended him in his cell and kept him warm at night by sleeping on his chest, leaving during the day to hunt down pigeons which it brought back to the imprisoned man to eat. You can still see a small memorial in Boxley Church in Kent, which Sir Henry had erected in gratitude to his feline friend.

Another English nobleman, Henry Wriothsley, 3rd Earl of Southampton, was also delighted to be joined by his faithful cat when he was imprisoned in the Tower. The little black and white cat sneaked in down a chimney to keep him company and, when the earl was finally released by James I, he had his portrait painted with his faithful companion alongside him.

Ray Thomas of Cleveland, Ohio, owes his life to Woodie, a collie mix owned by his fiancée, Rae Anne Knitter. In 1980 the threesome were walking along a nature trail in the Rocky River Reservation. Ray was a keen amateur photographer and saw a spectacular view he wanted to capture. Rae Anne and Woodie waited while Ray climbed a steep, shale cliff to get his shot. He'd only just disappeared from view when the usually well-behaved Woodie started tugging on his lead as if trying to break free.

Rae Anne couldn't hold him and, bursting free, Woodie raced up the slope after Ray with his owner scrambling behind him, calling him to come back. When Rae Anne reached the top of the cliff she saw her fiancee lying unconscious in a stream, eighty feet below. By his side was Woodie, who'd dived in and was nudging Ray's head to keep it above the fast flowing water. Although both Ray and Woodie were badly injured (Woodie broke both hips when he jumped), they have made full recoveries. In honour of his bravery, Woodie received the Dog Hero of the Year Award.

When Roz Brown collapsed and started slipping into a diabetic coma, her West Highland terrier, Holly, knew just what to do. She raced across the room, grabbed a bag of jelly babies and dropped the sweets in front of Roz's face. When Roz still didn't stir, Holly frantically nuzzled the back of her neck until she regained consciousness enough to reach two of the jelly babies. The sweets revived her by raising her blood sugar levels again.

'Holly is very intelligent, but she has never done anything as clever as this before,' said Roz afterwards. 'I often have a jelly baby if I'm feeling unwell and Holly must have seen me eating them.' She added, 'It's amazing she didn't eat any herself – she's mad about them!'

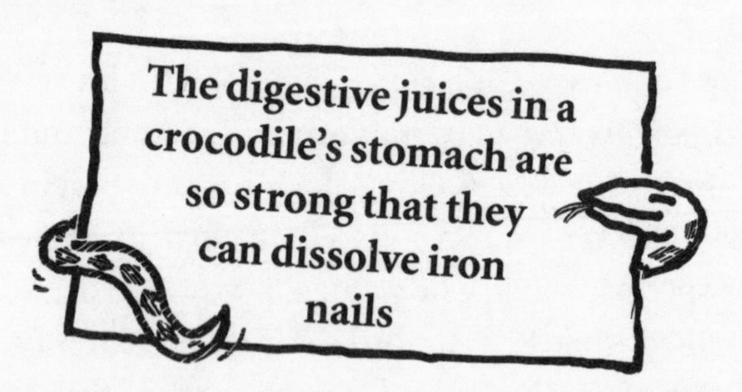


In May 1978, four fishermen became hopelessly lost in a dense fogbank off Dassen Island, South Africa. To their surprise, their boat was suddenly surrounded by dolphins, furiously swimming around and around the boat. The skipper took it as an omen to change course – and he was right. Just ahead was a treacherous shoal of jagged rocks, hidden in the fog.

The dolphins continued to bump and nudge the boat until it was in calmer waters, and refused to leave it alone until the grateful fishermen dropped anchor. Then they swam away. As the fog lifted, the four fishermen saw to their amazement that they were back in the very bay they had set out from. The dolphins had guided them safely home in the fog.

Real-life Goldilocks, five-year-old Goranka Cuculic, had an amazing story to tell when she was found wandering in a forest near her home in Vranje in the former Yugoslavia. She told rescuers that she had been befriended by three wild bears! 'One was big and fat, and the other two were quite small and as cuddly as they make them,' she said. 'I played in a meadow with the two small ones and shared my biscuits with them. The big one licked my face . . . its tongue tickled no end. At night I snuggled up between the cubs and was beautifully warm. The next day I somehow lost my teddy bears and I was glad when Uncle Ivan found me and I hope I meet them again!'

Mrs Candelaria Villanueva had one of the luckiest escapes of all time when the ferry she was on caught fire and sank between two islands in the Philippines. She was in the water for more than twelve hours and was on the verge of giving up, when a giant turtle suddenly surfaced directly under her, lifting her above the waves. A second, smaller turtle climbed on to her back. 'The small turtle bit me gently every time I felt drowsy,' she said. 'Maybe it wanted to prevent me from submerging my head in the water and drowning.'

Rescuers spotted Mrs Villanueva some 36 hours later. A Philippines naval vessel swept in to pick her up. One of the naval officers said, 'We thought she was clinging to an old oil drum. We didn't realise it was a giant turtle until we started hauling up the woman, for the turtle was beneath her, apparently propping her up. It even circled the area twice before disappearing into the depths of the sea, as if to reassure itself that its former rider was in good hands.'

Lom Yang-Yong, a South Korean sailor, also owes his life to a giant turtle! He fell overboard from his ship in the Bay of Bengal, grabbed hold of a passing turtle and clung on to it until his crew mates found him some six hours later. Using a crane, they pulled both the sailor and the turtle out of the sea – and gave the turtle a sumptuous meal of meat and bananas before returning him safely to the ocean. 'The turtle was very friendly. It did not hurt me at all,' Mr Lom said of his rescuer.

Bo was a Labrador retriever who loved the water. In 1892 she was rafting on the Colorado River with her owners, Laurie and Rob Roberts of Glenwood Spring, Colorado, and one of her puppies, Duchess.

All was going well until a sudden eight-foot wave crashed down on the raft, flipping it over. Rob and Duchess were thrown free, but Bo and Laurie were trapped underneath, fighting for breath as they were swept over rocks. Bo soon emerged, but instead of paddling away, she took a deep gulp of air and dived back under the raft, pulling Laurie free by her hair. Once she was free of the raft, Laurie held tightly on to Bo's tail as the dog swam in the fierce, swirling eddies, striking out for the river bank and fighting the strong current every inch of the way.

Eventually they reached the bank and hauled themselves out, exhausted, but both very much alive.

When a massive cyclone hit the coastal village of Chakoria in Bangladesh in 1991, a tiny baby was swept out to sea. A dolphin grabbed the baby and gripped him in his mouth, holding him safely up out of the water until rescuers could reach him. The dolphin let the rescuers take the baby from his mouth and then swam off.

It was Bitsy to the rescue when the schnauzer's elderly owner had a heart attack at the wheel of his car on a motorway in Houston, Texas. The dog jumped into the driving seat, knocked the steering wheel over to steer the car on to the hard shoulder and bit his owner's leg to remove it from the accelerator. Bitsy's owner, Jesus Martinez, later recovered in hospital.

When 75-year-old Jack Fyfe was paralysed by a stroke at his home in Eastwood, Western Sydney, his pet sheepdog, Trixie, helped him to stay alive. For nine days six-year-old Trixie brought him water by soaking a towel in her water bowl and draping it over his face so that he could suck it. When the bowl ran dry, Trixie improvised and used water from the toilet. Her actions undoubtedly saved Jack's life. He was eventually found by his daughter and taken to hospital.

Wilhelm Stachovski saved Bruno the dog's life – and Bruno returned the compliment. The retired postman intervened when he saw Bruno being attacked by a gang of thugs. He took the battered dog home, and slowly nursed him back to health. From that day on, the two became inseparable, and Wilhelm, who had been a recluse up till then, became more friendly and extroverted with the people he met. Some time later, people at the cafe where Bruno and Wilhelm always had lunch were alarmed to see Bruno running up on his own, barking furiously. The dog grabbed the cafe owner by his clothes and physically tried to drag him along the street. The owner understood and followed the dog back to Wilhelm's cottage, where he found the old man slumped helplessly in a chair, complaining of severe chest pains. An ambulance was called and Wilhelm was whisked off to hospital, where his life was saved.

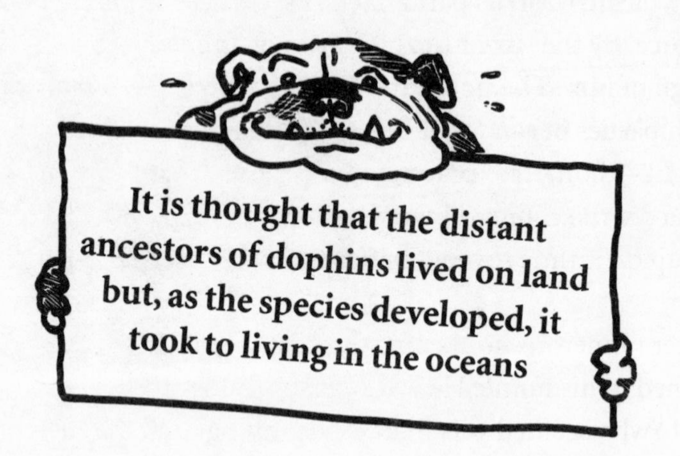


In 1992, a Danish farmer named Alf With lost his footing and fell over a treacherous cliff, ending up on a narrow ledge some 50 metres below the cliff edge. Somehow, his red setter, Tony, scrambled down the almost sheer face of the cliff after him and cuddled up to him on the ledge, keeping him warm for sixteen hours before a rescue helicopter located them and took them both off the cliffside. As soon as Alf got out of hospital, the first thing he did was to go to the butcher's shop and bring Tony home every single sausage in the shop!

In 1983, three-year-old Oscar Simonet got lost while on a picnic with his parents near their home in Villacarlos, Menorca. By the time his parents noticed he was gone, there was no sign of him. The police were called and hastily arranged search parties began to comb the desolate clifftops. Everyone thought – though no one wanted to say it – that little Oscar had fallen over the cliff and been swept out to sea. Instead, everyone gave up their time to search, including the town's mayor, Jose Tadeo.

After numerous hours out searching, the mayor finally returned to his home. He was met at the door by his Irish setter, Harpo, who seemed very agitated. Ignoring him, the mayor pulled off his boots and tried to sit down – but Harpo wasn't having it. He kept whining, yelping and barking, scratching at the front door and looking back at Jose. Intrigued, Jose got up and followed his dog out of the house. Harpo took him two miles across the cliffs to the exact spot where the little boy had disappeared. He started sniffing around, then furiously digging in a thick tangle of bushes the search party had skirted. Jose followed his dog in and found a hidden three-foot deep crevasse. The boy was lying inside, semi-conscious. He'd crawled into the undergrowth and dropped down out of sight.

Somehow, Harpo knew where he was – and that he was in trouble – and was absolutely determined to save the day!

## *Chapter Twelve*

# FANTASTIC JOURNEYS

Most incredible journeys are undertaken by dogs and cats, but cows are also capable of these fantastic feats. Daisy was a Friesian that was parted from her calf when she was sold at an auction in Okehampton in Devon. She was so unhappy that she escaped from her new owner's farm by jumping a gate, then trekked six miles across fields and through hedgerows to find her baby. Her new owner was so taken by Daisy's show of devotion that there was only one thing he could do – he bought the calf as well.

A family on holiday in upper New York State befriended a stray cat they called Daisy. Reluctantly, when the holiday was over they left her behind and returned to their home in New York City. A month later, they were stunned to find Daisy on their doorstep, carrying a tiny kitten in her mouth. She left again – only to return later with another kitten, and then another, and another, and then another. The family, needless to say, immediately adopted Daisy and her five kittens whom they had been feeding in the meantime.

Chester the tortoise took an immediate dislike to his new owner, eight-year-old Malcolm Edwards, when he was brought to the family home in Lyde, Hertfordshire. Despite having a big white cross painted on his shell to make him stand out in the long grass, Chester quickly disappeared and was given up for lost. Thirty-five years later, Malcolm's neighbour found a tortoise crawling along a grass verge near the village church – and Malcolm, now 43 years old, recognised the faded paint mark on Chester's back. In thirty-five years, Chester the tortoise had travelled an epic 750 yards – across to a copse, round to the bus stop and up to the village church.

Byrtle the turtle did a whole lot better. In the ten years following his escape from his pen in Long Beach, California, he managed to stroll over 200 miles from his home.

Just in case you think all tortoises and turtles are lazy and unambitious, Rosita, a loggerhead turtle, was tagged by the University of Arizona in 1994 and released from Baja, California, in July that year. In November 1995 she turned up again, 6,500 miles away off the coast of Kyushu, Japan, where she was found by a Japanese fisherman. This amazing journey –

almost a third of the way round the world – is thought to be the longest migration of any sea animal. Scientists now believe that loggerhead turtles actually hatched in Japan, migrate to California and then swim back to Japan to nest – a round trip of 13,000 miles.

On 9 May, 1962, a young Guernsey cow called Fawn was grazing peacefully in her field in Scott County, Iowa, when she was suddenly snatched up into the air by a passing tornado. She flew for over a mile-and-a-half before touching down safely in a neighbour's paddock. Five years after her maiden flight, the unlucky cow was once again swept up in a tornado. Passengers on a nearby bus saw her lifted clean up into the air, flying high over their heads before coming in for a perfect four-point landing on the far side of the road. After that, her owner took no more chances. If there was ever so much as a stiff breeze, Fawn was locked away in the barn. None the worse for her record-breaking flights, Fawn lived to the ripe old age of twenty-five.

In 1904, a thoroughbred South African racehorse called Moifaa was entered for the English Grand National. He was put aboard a ship for England and set sail – straight into the midst of one of the worst storms in living memory. The ship foundered, pitching Moifaa into the giant waves. The racehorse struck out and swam an incredible 100 miles to reach the coast of South Africa. You might think that, after this, Moifaa would be given a break but, no, his owners decided to ship him straight out again to run in the National. When news of his adventures reached the British gambling fraternity, they didn't think much of his chances of even completing the race and bookies gave him unflattering odds of 25-1. Moifaa proved them wrong by not only finishing but by romping home the clear winner!

Truck driver Geoff Hancock only stopped for a quick cup of coffee at a cafe, near Darwin, Australia, in October 1973 – but it was enough time for his little fox-terrier, Whisky, to jump out of the cab and get himself lost. Nine months later, Whisky came home to Melbourne, after a journey of almost 1,800 miles!

Owney the stray mongrel loved to ride on top of post office mail bags – and quickly became a well known face on board mail trains and at post offices throughout America at the end of the last century. Owney was seen as a good luck charm. No mail train he rode was ever derailed or held up and robbed, so post office staff indulged his whims and let him travel wherever he wanted to go. To keep track of him and to find out where he went, employees started to fix metallic baggage labels to his collar. He collected so many tags from across America that the postmaster general presented him with a special coat for displaying them all. Perhaps inspired by this, Owney decided to venture further afield. He soon turned up back at his 'home post office' in Albany with tags from Canada and Mexico! Knowing his love for travel, the post office sorters decided to send Owney on the round-the-world trip of a lifetime. From Tacoma, Washington, he set sail with the mail to Yokohama, Shanghai, Woosung, Foochow, Hong Kong, Singapore, Suez, Algiers and the Azores before returning to

America! Before he died, Owney notched up an incredible total of 143,000 miles and 1,017 baggage tags which he wore with pride. His jacket and tags can now be seen at the Smithsonian Institute's Museum of American History in Washington, DC.

Gato the tabby is adventurous, but not particularly bright. When the Humphreys family set off on holiday, they thought he was safely indoors. Wrong. He had, in fact, hidden himself on top of the luggage on the roofrack. The stowaway wasn't discovered until the family was about to board the Isle of Wight ferry, where staff spotted the cat still clinging on. He had travelled on the roof of the car for over one hundred miles!

**The average tuna swims one million miles in its lifetime – or the equivalent of travelling around the world about forty times**

Top security at a British nuclear power plant was breached in April 1996 not by a crack team of saboteurs – but by a 300lb seal named Lear.

Lear had managed to pass through a security grating at the Dungeness B power station on the south Kent coast and had swum along a supply pipe, finally surfacing in a 90-foot chamber inside the nuclear plant. She was spotted by technicians, who declared a full-scale emergency, calling on the RSPCA, Sea Life Centres in Sussex and Norfolk and the British Divers Marine Life Rescue Team.

A fierce whirlpool in the tank, caused by water rushing through at a rate of 500,000 gallons a minute, made it too dangerous to risk divers, or even an inflatable boat, so a crane was used to lower a diving platform with a large net spread across it.

The theory was that Lear would eventually have to take a break from swimming round and round – at which point the net would look a very attractive proposition. But Lear had more stamina than the plant officials had credited her with. She swam and swam . . . and swam. Gradually, other plans were starting to be drawn up, including shutting the whole plant down at an estimated cost of £500,000 per day!

72 hours after Lear had entered the tank, she began to flag and hauled herself onto the platform. She was then winched to safety and taken to the RSPCA hospital in Norfolk where she was given a clean bill of health – and released back into the sea near the Wash.

Alan Knight was head of the diving team that organised Lear's recovery. He told the press, 'We've tried to capture a Beluga whale in the Black Sea, we've released dolphins from captivity in Britain out in the Caribbean, but this is the most unusual rescue we have ever done . . . and the hardest.'

Migrating toads may not have to travel very far to get back to their spawning ponds, but their journeys are fraught with danger, not least the problem of busy roads. You'll be pleased to hear then that at least one road in the UK has now been made 'toad-friendly'. In the past, the busy A283 London Road in Petworth, Sussex, has been such a toad accident blackspot that local people have come out to personally conduct the migrating toads across the road. Now, however, planners have installed a special Toad Tunnel under the road. The amphibian underpass is proving a great success, and only one toad casualty has been reported since the tunnel was built.

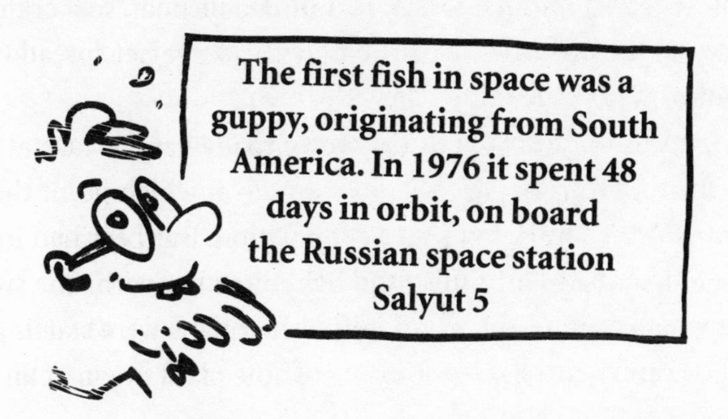


A two-year-old cream-coloured Persian cat named Sugar was born with a hip deformity and this made her very uncomfortable whenever she travelled by road. When her owner, Stacy Wood, retired in 1952, he moved with his wife from their home town of Anderson in California to Gage in Oklahoma. They decided that it would be for the best if Sugar was left with a close neighbour, rather than suffer the long car journey.

Two weeks after they left, Sugar disappeared – only to reappear fourteen months later at her owners' new house – a place she had never even seen! Mrs Wood was working in the barn of their new home when she felt something leap onto her back. Instinctively, she knocked it away – and was stunned to see it was Sugar.

To cover the 1,500-mile journey meant that Sugar had travelled over 100 miles a month, across the great American desert and the Rocky Mountains – and that was with her bad hip. The case was so unbelievable that it was investigated by J B Rhine, a well-known American parapsychologist who, after examining the cat and talking to witnesses, validated Sugar's exploits, making her joint holder of the longest pussy pilgrimage.

When Paul Aspland of Norfolk brought Hamlet, the black and white cat, home with him from Toronto on a British Airways jumbo, it was a start of the adventure of a lifetime for the unfortunate cat. When the plane touched down at Heathrow, his cage door was wide open and there was no sign of him. A thorough search of the entire aircraft revealed no trace of the missing moggy.

Almost two months later, a routine maintenance check uncovered Hamlet safe and sound behind some panelling. He had flown all around the world and visited Jamaica, Kuwait, Singapore and Australia – a journey of some 600,000 air miles!

In 1995, a debate erupted in the revered pages of *New Scientist* magazine, about whether or not pigeons were using the London Underground to travel about the capital. Readers sent in their observations of pigeons either singly or in pairs jumping on tube trains, strutting around the carriage and then getting off at the next stop, as if they knew where they were gong. Reports said that the pigeons were not interested in food offered to them by amused commuters – a very strange fact in itself – they simply wanted to travel. The most popular destinations for passenger pigeons are, according to the magazine, apparently Baker Street and Goldhawk Road stations!

According to a letter to *The Times* newspaper in September 1985, pigeons were taking particular advantage of the london Underground District Line, waddling on board trains at Edgware Road station and getting off at subsequent stations as they travel south. One reader observed that the birds, 'alight at various points along the line. Fulham Broadway and Parson's Green seem to be favoured and also Putney Bridge if it is low water.'

On 23 June, 1985, Barbara Paule was driving her truck in Dayton, Ohio, accompanied by her cat, Muddy Water White. For whatever reason, while the vehicle was stationary, Muddy decided to jump out and was soon out of sight. Barbara never replaced him, but exactly three years later a stray appeared at her house in Pennsylvania and flopped down on her doorstep. She took him in – but it was only after three days that she realised that this scraggy newcomer was in fact none other than Muddy Water White, a fact verified by the local vet who identified him; he'd travelled 450 miles, in an epic journey lasting over 1,000 days, to get home.

When John Sutcliffe opened his front door one day in August 1973, he was greeted by a tiny, thin ginger kitten on his doorstep. It looked familiar and his wife recognised it immediately. It was the exact same kitten that she'd given her granddaughter about three weeks earlier. This little kitten had found its way back home after walking over 150 miles.

Although dogs and cats have covered incredible distances in a short period of time, the opposite is also true.

A Siamese cat called Ching disappeared while she and her owners were on holiday at a caravan site at Ammanford in

South Wales in 1967. She eventually arrived back at the family home at Stow-on-the-Wold in Gloucestershire three years later, during which time she'd ambled along at a leisurely rate of 175 yards a day.

Neptune the dog tracked his owners over fifty miles. Now that might not seem like a long way given some of the other tales, but Neptune swam all the way – against the tide. Neptune was a Newfoundland dog, a breed known for their swimming abilities. He was on board a boat being towed up the Mississippi on the way to New Orleans when the vessel listed violently, tipping him into the water. The captain couldn't stop his boat since it was being towed and had to watch sadly as Neptune was left behind, unable to keep up.

Rather than swim ashore, Neptune decided to follow the boat in the distance. Three days later, to the amazement of the captain and all the crew, he swam alongside. He'd tracked them to New Orleans against strong tides and bad weather – and jumped on board as if nothing was wrong.

## *Chapter Thirteen*

# Them and Us

Mr Snowy Farr of Cambridge raised nearly £30,000 for charity and donated seventeen guide dogs, by performing in Cambridge's market square every Saturday for over ten years. His act? Well it consisted of Mr Farr's cat sitting on top of his top hat and his mice running round and round the brim – a good time being had by all.

About his act, Mr Farr said, 'Only God, myself and my animals tell me what to do, and that's how it all started.'

The residents of Jaboata in Brazil were so fed up with their corrupt and lazy local government that in 1955 they actually ran a goat for mayor. A goat named Smelly. Surprisingly, (or perhaps not, in the volatile world of Brazilian politics), the goat won with a 468-vote majority.

There must be something about Brazilians and local politics because four years later, in 1959, the residents of São Paulo in Brazil voted a female rhinoceros called Cacareo onto the council. This was done as a protest vote against the high cost of living and food shortages. Cacareo won by a landslide 50,000 votes, and she appeared on the front page of the *New York Times.* Unfortunately, Cacaero was banned from taking her place, in a prime example of blatent rhinocerosism. Although the vote was made null and void, the residents took comfort in the fact that they'd made a political statement.

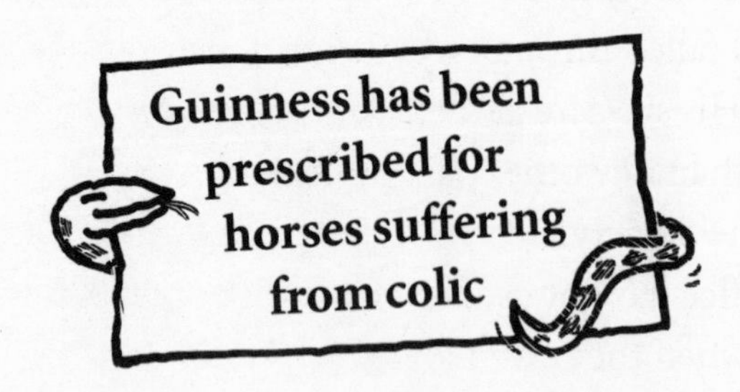


Daisy, Daphne, Denise, Daffy and Donald are five of the most pampered guests at the prestigious Peabody Hotel in Memphis, Tennessee. They live together in the penthouse suite, but as you've probably guessed from their names, they're not people – but ducks. Mallards, to be precise.

Their story begins fifty years ago when the then-manager of the hotel (a duck fan), bought a few to liven up the fountain in the hotel lobby. Since then the ducks have become something of an institution and a tradition that's been maintained.

They might have plush accommodation and good food (room service delivers grain, carrots, cabbage tops and lettuce) but they have to work for it. The ducks' routine starts at 7am every day when they go down to the lobby in the lift. They are escorted along a red carpet in single file, accompanied by a guard of honour of bellboys. They are then ushered into the ornate marble fountain where they spend all day swimming about. Guests love the sight and it provides the ducks with exercise.

Every few months the ducks leave the hotel to relax on a farm outside Memphis. While they're there, resting their little webbed feet, a replacement five ducks are brought in. The replacements are hatched on the same farm and it's said that they're the descendants of the original Peabody ducks.

The British Hedgehog Preservation Society has a membership of over 5,000. It was founded by Major Adrian Coles who'd cared for hedgehogs ever since he rescued one that had fallen through a cattle grid near his home in Shropshire. His six-acre garden once boasted more hedgehogs per hectare than any other part of the country. Although based in Britain, the Society receives letters from all over the world. The Post Office has got used to the way people address letters to the Society when they don't know its proper address: 'Major Hedgehog, England'.

Dismayed by falling attendances at their greyhound races, in 1937 the owners of Romford Greyhound Stadium tried a bold new attraction – cheetah racing. With cheetahs able to reach speeds of 70 miles per hour over short distances, the attraction seemed certain to pull the crowds. Unfortunately, as soon as one cheetah got into the lead, all the others simply gave up. Bets were then made on the speed of a single cheetah running alone. However, the single cheetah almost immediately worked out that all he had to do was lie on the track and wait for the rabbit to come around to him . . . cheetah racing has never been tried again.

Before the Berlin Wall was demolished a West German cat named Putzi climbed up it and over the top into East Germany. Its distraught owner wanted to climb over and rescue him but was threatened with shooting by the border guards. He got Putzi back though. While his children distracted the guards, the owner drilled a small hole in the wall and Putzi climbed through.

By the way, a cow once defected from East to West Germany by swimming 150 yards across the River Elbe. She was granted asylum in the West.

Emilio Tarra was driving along a deserted stretch of the road between Perth and Adelaide when a kangaroo suddenly jumped out in front of him. Emilio, a crew member on an America's Cup yacht, swerved, but still couldn't miss the kanga. He stopped, got out and took a look at the dead roo. Then, for some reason best known to himself, he decided to dress it up in his expensive Gucci blazer and take a souvenir photograph. Serves him right. The kangaroo wasn't dead, just stunned. It knocked him flat on his back and bounded off into the bush still wearing Emilio's blazer which, by the way, contained his passport, sixteen credit cards and $2,000 Australian dollars in cash. Should've tied that kangaroo down.

A gorilla in a Florida zoo certainly looked like a gorilla, but didn't act like one, preferring to spend its time near the bars of its enclosure, eavesdropping on conversations nearby.

Could it understand what people were talking about? You bet it could! The gorilla was actually an FBI agent in a monkey suit. He was investigating the alleged smuggling of primates from Miami to Mexico – and caught the zoos and parks director for Mexico red-handed, arranging a $90,000 deal!

Ghanaian master criminal John Ofosu had a very unusual way of stealing goats. He would dress them up as people and drive off with them in his battered old Ford Escort. Police finally apprehended him when he was flagged down for speeding. 'I thought the family in the car were all very ugly,' said police officer Mustapha Garbah in court. 'Then I saw that the 14 people were all pregnant goats in T-shirts.'

When Amy Dougherty's boyfriend discovered that she suffered from a fear of spiders, he decided to help her overcome her fear by buying her a pet tarantula. She just about coped with this, and was even starting to be able to look at the tarantula without flinching when, without warning, it suddenly gave birth to 750 babies in its tank at her home in Bexhill, East Sussex.

A black bear, trapped sixty feet up a pine tree, brought chaos to the small town of Keithville, Kentucky, one night in February 1991. As a crowd gathered, sherriff's deputies, game wardens and wildlife experts debated the best way to get the bear down safely. A vet fired tranquilliser darts up at the unfortunate creature and the police strung a net around the tree, waiting to catch it when it fell. Eight hours later, the bear was still firmly up the tree. Having run out of options, the police decided to chop the tree down – and discovered that the bear they had been trying to rescue was just an old black bin liner . . .

*Pro-Rat-A* is the official magazine of the National Rat Fancy Society. It is packed with handy hints and tips for keeping your prized rodent happy and healthy, as well as containing adverts for rat-related products like keyrings and sweatshirts, a problem page and even a rat obituary column.

The widow of a wealthy Australian fur dealer left a million dollars to a pair of polar bears in Perth Zoo.

More often, people leave considerable sums of money to their pets. Brownie and Hellcat, two fifteen-year-old cats living in San

Diego had something to purr about; they were left $400,000 by their owner in the 1960s. After the cats themselves had passed away in 1965 their trustee donated the remaining monies, on their behalf, to a Washington university.

Slightly less well-off, but still comfortable, was Sarah, a goat living in Kentucky. She inherited $115,000 from her owner's estate.

161 Dogs, belonging to oil heiress Eleanor Ritchley, shared her will of $4.3 million, while a German shepherd with the grand name of Viking Baron von Heppeplatz was left an entire apartment block in Munich when his master died in 1971 . . . Toby the Poodle was left the equivalent of £15 million in a will when his owner, Miss Ella Wendel of New York, died in 1931. During his life he slept on silk sheets in his own room, had breakfast served in bed each morning and had his own personal butler always in attendance.

Closer to home, twelve-year-old Minky the cat was left £10,000 in her owner's will in 1986, 'to keep her in style for the rest of her life'. The trustees were bound to provide a daily menu for her which included a choice of dishes such as chicken served with a side portion of chopped livers and poached cod in a parsley sauce.

One of the best stories about wealthy animals involved a sheepdog called William. William belonged to London investment analyst Robert Beckman who opened a share trading account in his name when the dog was a puppy. Under William's name he traded on the stock exchange, stipulating that only William could have access to the profits. He'd soon amassed a fortune of over £100,000 on his dog's behalf. The Inland Revenue heard about this and tried to claim Capital Gains Tax of £30,000, first from Beckman, then the dog and his owner, jointly. After a long court battle they finally admitted defeat in February 1985 and reluctantly dropped their action.

The eccentric French playwright Gerard de Nerval could often be seen taking his pet lobster for a walk on a leash. When normal Parisiennes asked him why, he replied, 'Because it does not bark and it knows the secrets of the sea.'

In Somerset, Twelfth Night used to be considered a holy day of rest for working animals. Horses and cattle got the day off and kindly owners would sneak special presents into their troughs. Top of Santa's list for cows, apparently, was salted herring.

On a stormy night at the turn of this century, a brilliant young surgeon at the New York Hospital for Specialist Surgery, Dr Brian Gibney, made his housecall. He got a message that someone had broken their leg in a fall and that medical help was required immediately. But when Gibney arrived at the huge greystone mansion that belonged to John Wendle and his seven spinster sisters, he couldn't believe his eyes. He'd been called out in an emergency – for a poodle called Toby.

But when you consider the Wendle family and their eccentricities, this wasn't that unusual. John Wendle had amassed a fortune from real estate, but he and his sisters rarely left the house. The sisters feared fortune hunters and kept well out of the way of men behind the house's huge walls. John believed that dye used in clothing was bad for your health. As a result he had all his suits woven from the wool of pure black sheep.

Now, the sisters might have hated men but they loved dogs, particularly poodles. Each dog slept in its own specially-made, hand-carved miniature four-poster bed and ate tender lamb chops. After Dr Gibney had got over first his shock, and then his annoyance, he proceeded to treat Toby as if he were human. He examined the fracture, set it and visited the dog regularly over the following months until the leg had healed. Toby lead a full active life again and Dr Gibney never heard from the Wendles again. That is, until the last sister died years later. It seems they were so grateful to Dr Gibney for helping poor Toby, they left his hospital a multi-million-dollar legacy in their will. This went towards the hospital's new building – a nice way of remembering dear old Toby.

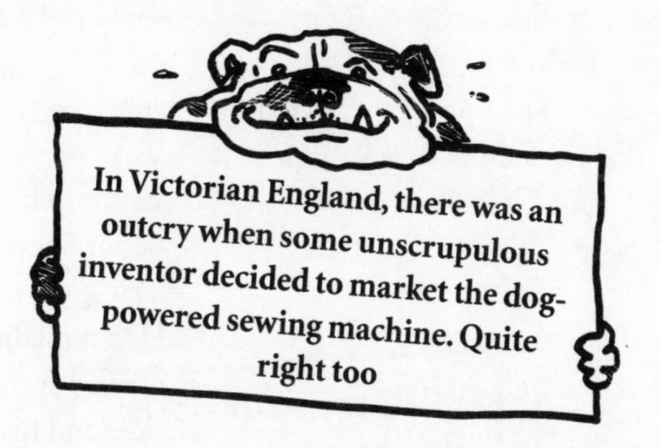


There aren't many pigs that have their own custom-built brick house complete with a chimney (so Father Christmas can deliver his presents) and lacy curtains – but then there aren't many pigs like Ben.

Ben's house is called 'Pigmalion' and is at the Sanctuary for Injured Animals in Gwent, Wales. He was adopted by Maria Hennesey and, over the years, Ben's fame has spread worldwide. He has his own fan club (Maria answers letters on his behalf – well, it's difficult to hold a pen in your trotter) and his own special diet. While his piggie brethren eat boring old grain, Ben has quite a varied vegetarian menu and washes each meal down with his favourite tipple – strawberry milkshake.

Cats are no trouble to look after, right? Well, imagine you had 689 of them living with you. That's right, six hundred and eighty nine. That's the total cat population in the Wright household in Kingston, Ontario. Donna Wright has to get up every morning at 5.30 to start cleaning out the ten giant-sized litter trays. 154lb of kitty litter later, it's time to start the feeding process. Every day, Donna's cats munch their way through 180 giant-sized cans of meat and 55lb of dried cat food, and lap up ten and a half pints of full-cream milk! Donna makes sure that none are ignored, and there's always time for a fuss and a cuddle for any cat who wants one. When the day is done, at least thirty of the more sociable cats bed down with Donna in the master bedroom.

The cats are all strays. They each have their own name and Donna and her husband Jack swear that they can tell you which one is which!

Great ideas that never took off No. 410: a Devon adventure park announced that it was going to be offering exciting 'sheep races' as a major new tourist attraction. They already had twelve sheep in training, said a spokesman, including Red Ram, Sheargar and Alderknitti . . .

In 1803, the Reverend Robert Stephen Hawker excommunicated a cat for catching a mouse during Sunday service. Nine other, better-behaved, cats attending the service were allowed to stay.

The Auckland Safari Park used to look after banknotes belonging to a local New Zealand bank by keeping them in the tiger's cage – up to $50,000 was kept overnight. This worked well for two weeks, but when the notes were returned to the bank the cash smelled of tiger sweat – and of other bodily odours . . .

The notes had to be sprayed with deodorant before customers would take them, and even then the smell lingered for days. This new concept in security was soon abandoned.

Now I know why Santa always uses reindeer. It wasn't very seasonal, but it was certainly pretty spectacular when the Cavendish Hotel in Eastbourne decided to have Santa arrive on his sleigh . . . drawn by an elephant. It was also asking for trouble.

Lola, the five-year-old elephant standing in for Rudolph, ran amok and careered around the streets with Santa clinging on for dear life! She tipped the sleigh over, burst free of her reins, barged into two cars, denting them badly, and finally smashed through the front doors of an adjoining hotel scattering guests in all directions before drawing to a halt in the lobby.

The hotel manager explained later, 'A wheel of the sleigh got caught on the kerb as it came around the corner and the noise spooked Lola. The sleigh broke into bits and Santa fell off.'

During the 1996 general election in India, one candidate trained a host of parrots to squawk his name and then released them into the surrounding countryside. 'It's very important to get your name known,' he said.